"**Every time you** ~~n~~ **feel something** ~~pull~~ **back.**"

"A bodyguard getting involved with his subject would put her at risk."

Moving closer, Lynn stared up into his face which he'd schooled into a neutral expression. "Is that the real reason, Blade? Is it?"

"We should get back to work," Blade said, though he didn't make a move to open the door.

"Why? Are you afraid to talk about it?" Lynn didn't care—she wanted answers. She wanted something that explained why she opened herself to a man she barely knew. Why she wanted more. "You say you care about me—how much?"

"More than makes me comfortable."

Moving so close there was barely breathing room, she murmured, "Maybe we're not supposed to get too comfortable with each other."

With a groan, Blade snaked an arm behind her back and pulled her up against him. Lynn gasped, but before she could take another breath, his mouth crushed hers in a torrid kiss.

Dear Harlequin Intrigue Reader,

This month Harlequin Intrigue has a healthy dose of breathtaking romantic suspense to reignite you after the cold winter days. Kicking things off, Susan Kearney delivers the first title in her brand-new trilogy HEROES INC., based on a specially trained team of sexy agents taking on impossible missions. In *Daddy to the Rescue,* an operative is dispatched to safeguard his ex-wife from the danger that threatens her. Only, now he also has to find the child she claims is his!

Rebecca York returns with the latest installment in her hugely popular 43 LIGHT STREET series. *Phantom Lover* is a supersexy gothic tale of suspense guaranteed to give you all kinds of fantasies.... Also appearing this month is another veteran Harlequin Intrigue author, Patricia Rosemoor, with the next title in her CLUB UNDERCOVER miniseries. In *VIP Protector,* a bodyguard must defend a prominent attorney from a crazed stalker. But can he protect her from long-buried secrets best left hidden?

Finally rounding out the month is the companion title in our MEN ON A MISSION theme promotion, *Tough as Nails,* from debut author Jackie Manning. Here an estranged couple must join forces to solve a deadly mystery, but will their close proximity fuel the flames of passion smoldering between them?

So pick up all four of these thrilling, action-packed stories for a full course of unbelievable excitement!

Sincerely,

Denise O'Sullivan
Senior Editor
Harlequin Intrigue

VIP PROTECTOR

PATRICIA ROSEMOOR

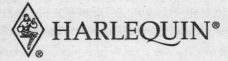

TORONTO • NEW YORK • LONDON
AMSTERDAM • PARIS • SYDNEY • HAMBURG
STOCKHOLM • ATHENS • TOKYO • MILAN • MADRID
PRAGUE • WARSAW • BUDAPEST • AUCKLAND

ISBN 0-373-22707-8

VIP PROTECTOR

Copyright © 2003 by Patricia Pinianski

This edition published by arrangement with Harlequin Books S.A.

® and TM are trademarks of the publisher. Trademarks indicated with ® are registered in the United States Patent and Trademark Office, the Canadian Trade Marks Office and in other countries.

Visit us at www.eHarlequin.com

Printed in U.S.A.

ABOUT THE AUTHOR

To research her novels, Patricia Rosemoor is willing to swim with dolphins, round up mustangs or howl with wolves—"whatever it takes to write a credible tale." She's the author of contemporary, historical and paranormal romances, but her first love has always been romantic suspense. She won both a *Romantic Times* Career Achievement Award in Series Romantic Suspense and a Reviewer's Choice Award for one of her more than thirty Intrigue novels. She's now writing erotic thrillers for Harlequin Blaze.

She would love to know what you think of this story. Write to Patricia Rosemoor at P.O. Box 578297, Chicago, IL 60657-8297 or via e-mail at Patricia@PatriciaRosemoor.com, and visit her Web site at http://PatriciaRosemoor.com.

Books by Patricia Rosemoor

HARLEQUIN INTRIGUE

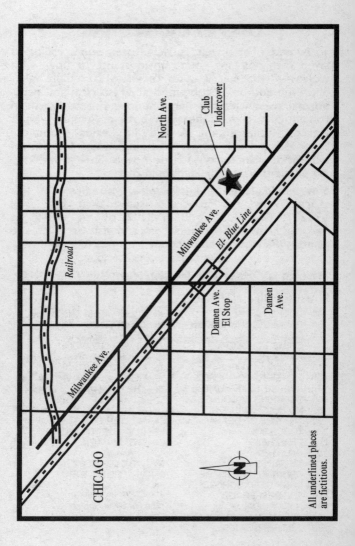

CHICAGO

North Ave.

Club
Undercover

Milwaukee Ave.

El- Blue Line

Railroad

Milwaukee Ave.

Damen Ave.
El Stop

Damen
Ave.

N

All underlined places
are fictitious.

CAST OF CHARACTERS

Lynn Cross—The high-profile divorce attorney was determined to reveal which of her client's husbands held her prisoner and threatened her with death.

Blade Stone—The ex-Special Forces military man would protect Lynn with his life—the least he could do, considering the secret he was hiding.

Timothy Cooper—After losing his wife, the macabre chef told Lynn that he'd kill her.

Victor Churchill—Once Lynn landed a huge settlement for the CEO's wife, he promised to ruin her.

Johnny Rincon—When the bully and gang leader from Blade's old neighborhood lost his favorite punching bag, he informed Lynn she would be getting what she deserved.

Nathan Sennet—Determined to get his wife back, Lynn's ex-brother-in-law accused her of making assumptions when she interfered in his life.

Roger Wheeler—After being banned from seeing his own children until he got counseling, the abusive cop told Lynn that if he had his way, she'd regret the day she'd been born.

To Edward, for our twenty years of marriage
and for your twenty years of being a writer's husband
with all that entails.

Prologue

"Please…why are you doing this?"

More croaked than articulated, her question—asked dozens of times now—still went unanswered. Oh, he'd spoken to her, whispered vague statements that hadn't made any sense. And as time had gone on, a feeling of doom had filled her.

She wanted to keep questioning him, to force him to reply, but her throat was so dry she could hardly swallow. Thankfully, he hadn't retaped her mouth shut as he'd threatened he would if she screamed again.

She *had* screamed, hadn't she?

How long ago?

Hours? Days?

Hard to remember now. Her head was spinning so badly that even if she could see, even if he hadn't tied a cloth around her eyes, she probably couldn't focus. As it was, her *mind* wouldn't focus, wouldn't settle on the one thing, the very important thing, that would tell her what had really happened, how she had gotten here, into this chair, hands tied behind her back…*a prisoner*. Her brain wouldn't focus on what she needed to do so that he would release her.

Then they flooded her. Memories of threats. *Death threats.* He'd been taunting her, threatening to kill her!

Not knowing why or how she could escape such a fate made her heart and her stomach race right up into her throat. At his mercy, she fought the fear and the bile…tried to concentrate…but her mind whirled.

Because he'd drugged her.

Some time ago, maybe when he'd gotten tired of her incessant questions, he'd held her jaw and made her drink. The taste of the liquid had been bitter and, fearing it was poison, she'd tried spitting out the foul stuff. But he'd hit her across the face, and then when he'd tried again, she'd been too stunned to fight him.

He'd made her drink more than once, hadn't he?

Who was he?

She could barely remember her own name.

Evelyn Cross. My name is Evelyn Cross.

She kept repeating this to herself over and over so that she wouldn't forget who she was.

He was moving around the room now. She could hear him, making noises as if he was preparing to do something so awful she couldn't even imagine what that might be. And she had a good imagination.

"Please…" She tried again. "Say *something!*"

"You're the one who does all the talking."

Unready for a direct response, even shrouded as it was in a whisper, Lynn started in surprise. She tried licking her lips but had no saliva. "Why?"

"Think about what you've done, Evelyn."

What *she* had done?

As if she were a child. A naughty child who needed to think about why she was being punished.

He'd said something about that before, only now she couldn't remember.

Think…think!

Bam, bam, bam!

Before the memory could gel, a loud hammering sound made her jump. Her chair rocked backward and threatened to spill her to the ground. She managed to keep from falling, but the inside of her head seemed to tumble into space.

Even so, she caught his low, grunted curse.

Bam, bam, bam!

"Open up. Police!"

Police?

"Help!" she rasped. "Help!"

More noise from inside the room. A window? She forced herself to concentrate as her captor spoke to her, his tone low and his voice breathy as if he were exerting himself.

"This is your fault. *Everything* is your fault. You got away with it this time, bitch. But you'll pay! Until we meet again…"

And then she sensed him slip away.

A crash and the splintering of wood told her the police had burst through the door, and she sobbed, "Thank God!"

"Police! Wherever you are, freeze!"

"No one's here but the woman," came a second, deeper voice.

"Check the bathroom."

She felt hands at the back of her head and sudden light exploded at her. She squeezed her eyes shut, then blinked them open, squinting hazily at what looked to be a seedy hotel room. Suddenly her hands were free, but she could barely move her arms. She focused on a uniform.

"Nothing in there, either."

"Window," she croaked, and the second police officer rushed around her.

"Too late. He's gone."

Gone but not forgotten, she thought hysterically. And he wouldn't forget her, either.

Whoever *he* was.

Until we meet again...

He would be back.

And then *she* would be dead.

Chapter One

"We'll get the bastard, Ms. Cross," Detective Stella Jacobek pronounced, her green eyes sympathetic. "It's only a matter of time."

Sitting up in the hospital bed, where she'd spent the last twenty-four hours coming out of her drugged stupor, Lynn stared at the woman, who looked to be her own age, barely approaching thirty.

Trying to keep her hand from shaking, she sipped from the cup of water on her tray—her third cupful since the interview began—and asked, "What if I don't have time? What if he's waiting for me when I get home?"

The detective closed her notebook and stuck her pen in the thick twist of golden-brown hair at the nape of her neck. "Maybe instead of going home, you might want to pick up a few things and go to a friend's house. Or maybe a relative's?"

Lynn shook her head. "I don't want to involve anyone else in this mess. You think you're in control, then something like this happens."

Her older sister had died violently nearly two years ago. Her younger sister was temporarily working in London, England, trying to heal from the wounds of a fresh divorce. Her parents, while still together, though God knew why, had problems of their own. Her father had been ill for some time and her mother had turned herself into his caretaker. Over the phone Evelyn had given them an edited version of what had happened to her, but no, she wouldn't involve them.

"Then I'll drive you home myself and check out your place personally, Ms. Cross."

"Lynn, please. I use Evelyn at work," she explained. Then she added, "My building has a security staff. No one can get in without their knowing it."

"Security. Good." The detective nodded approvingly. "And I'm Stella. I've gotta say I admire what you do."

"Splitting people up?"

"Nah, you don't do that. You just get the wives what they deserve."

"I didn't know anyone was paying attention."

"Who could miss the action on the Churchill case? It was front page news. But more important is your pro bono work—representing women who don't have the means to leave the men who mistreat them."

"A good reason for getting up in the morning."

"I've been thinking about what you said—that whoever did this was trying to punish you, that he said you're the one doing all the talking. You talk in court. Take away things from men. Sometimes violent men."

"I've been thinking the same thing. Plus he called me Evelyn," Lynn croaked.

Her throat was still sore, as were her wrists, and the side of her face where the bastard had hit her. She wasn't sure which was worse—being held captive or the aftermath, doctors probing her body for wounds, police penetrating her mind for answers. Not having been able to remember details, she'd had a thorough examination, including a pelvic. To her relief, she hadn't been raped.

"But if I had to name someone on the spot…" Not having a clue at the moment, Lynn shook her head.

"Let's give it some time. I'm sure you'll have some thoughts on it. Now go ahead and get dressed, and I'll wait for you out in the hall," the detective told her. "Unless you need help—"

"I don't need anyone." Defiantly, Lynn swung her legs over the edge of the bed. "I mean, I'm fine. No ill effects."

The other woman nodded again and left the room.

No ill effects…

Was that true?

Her head was clear, she was steady on her feet, her body parts all worked…but what about inside?

As she dressed, Evelyn caught a ghostly glimpse of herself in the window. On the surface, she looked the same—long, dark blond hair, nice features, health club body. But her eyes were different. The pale gray seemed to have darkened to steel. If eyes were truly the mirror to the soul, then her soul was deeply wounded.

And afraid.

Shuddering, she pulled on the clothes she'd been given, glad that they'd taken what she'd been wearing to forensics. She didn't want any reminder of the last two days.

According to their calculations, before another resident of the hotel had called the police after hearing her scream, her assailant had held her for about thirty-six hours.

Whoever *he* was.

Lynn decided she would forget him, too, then admitted the lie.

She would never forget.

Until we meet again...

Neither would he.

Taking a deep breath, she scraped back her messy hair and clipped it away from her face, then left the curtained alcove.

The drive home was tense. Despite the detective's best efforts to keep her engaged in conversation, Lynn felt herself slipping back to the abduction.

What had she done to bring that horror down on her?

And as they approached her building—a downtown high-rise on the Chicago River, overlooking Lake Michigan, she grew uneasy. Pulse pounding, she swept her gaze over every vehicle and every pedestrian in sight.

"See anything out of order?" Stella asked, pulling the car in front of Lynn's building.

"No, nothing. Still..."

"You're gonna sweat every time you leave or come home, at least for a while."

"Until you figure out who the bastard is, and arrest him."

"I can't do that until you give me something to go on. If you think of anything, come up with a name, you let me know. In the meantime, chances are this guy will never come anywhere near you."

Until we meet again...

With his threat echoing in her mind, Lynn muttered, "Yeah, right."

Maybe Stella *was* right, though. Maybe he'd been

bluffing. Lynn wanted to believe that. She needed to believe it if she was going to carry on with her life with any sense of normalcy.

Still…

She found herself looking over her shoulder as the other woman escorted her inside the building. They stopped at the security station, where Lynn introduced the detective to Tony Anselmo, the night guard, who had that morning's newspaper on his desk.

Seeing a photograph of herself on the front page, Lynn seethed as Stella gave the guard her card and told him she needed to talk with him, to ask a few questions, on her way out. If she was going to be front-page news, she wanted it to be because she'd won a big case, not because she was a victim.

"Sure. Anything I can do to help you nail this guy," Tony said, his expression sympathetic. "I'm just glad you're all right, Ms. Cross."

"Thanks, Tony," Lynn said, then rushed toward the waiting elevator.

She didn't want anyone's pity. She wasn't helpless. She was no victim…not normally.

As the elevator ascended to the twenty-eighth floor, Stella slipped her card out of her pocket. She scribbled something on the back. "Lynn, I'm going to give you my cell phone number just in case you have any concerns."

In case she saw her abductor, Lynn thought, taking the detective's contact information.

A sweep of her apartment—living room, bedroom, single bath, kitchen and a dining area with a lake view turned into a home office with desktop computer—didn't take long. Then, Detective Stella Jacobek headed on her way.

And Lynn was left alone with her thoughts.

Her bedroom overlooked the river, and normally the view through the glass wall soothed her. Lights lit the walkway and the fountain that shot a stream of water south across the river in a high arch. Farther east, Navy Pier beckoned with its giant Ferris wheel and tourist boats. But tonight she had difficulty feeling good about anything.

How could she when her abductor was still at large? She knew the man who'd kidnapped her could appear mild-mannered, even retiring. He could be anyone, anywhere…

A shrill sound made her jump. The phone. She started for it, then changed her mind. Whether the person at the other end was a reporter or a friend, she wasn't in the mood for questions. Not yet. She needed time to regroup, so she let the answering machine pick up.

"Cross residence," came her professional courtroom voice. *"We're too busy to pick up the phone right now, but we don't want to miss your call, so please leave your name and number and we'll get back to you as soon as we have a minute."*

Even though she didn't want to answer, Lynn couldn't help monitoring the call.

"We? Come on, Evelyn, who do you think you're fooling?" The familiar whispered voice paused for a second, then said, *"We both know you're alone. You're probably sitting there in the dark, terrified of your own shadow."*

Heart beating madly, she picked up the receiver and clapped it to her ear. "Who is this?"

Soft laughter was followed by his whispered response. "The one who's going to make sure you're punished for your misdeeds."

And with that he hung up.

Lynn screamed shrilly, clicked the off button and threw the receiver at the wall.

She wasn't drugged now, but her mouth was dry and she could hardly think. The bastard knew her home phone number. He probably knew where she lived, as well.

She wasn't going to wait for him to come get her.

Dragging a suitcase from the back of her closet, she set it on the bed. Then she opened her underwear drawer.

And the phone rang again.

Lynn froze and stared at the answering machine, her heart beating so loudly, she barely heard her voice answering.

"Lynn, this is Detective Jacobek. Stella."

Fully expecting the anonymous whisper, Lynn had trouble getting her legs to work properly. Picking up the phone, she said, "He called."

"When?"

"A few minutes ago." She balanced the receiver between her shoulder and ear and went back to packing. "I can't stay here. He'll get to me—"

"Don't do anything rash."

"Rash? Coming back here without protection was rash. Even as we speak I'm packing to correct that. I'm going to check into a hotel...or maybe I'll take the first flight to anywhere." Heading back to the closet to fetch a few pairs of slacks and her favorite designer jacket, Lynn said, "I have to get out of here."

"But maybe you won't have to go far," the detective proposed. "I just got a call from…well, I have a possible solution for you. Give me an hour."

"I can't—"

"An hour, Lynn, that's all I'm asking for. I'm going to find a solution away from the department. Unofficial."

Knowing the CPD didn't assign baby-sitters to potential victims, Lynn stopped and frowned. "Why would you do this for me?"

"Because a few months ago you helped someone I knew from the old neighborhood. One of your pro bono cases. Now I want to help you. And save that message for me. We might be able to do something with it in the lab."

The reasoning got to Lynn. "All right. I'll give you an hour," she agreed, though she wondered who had called and what this solution might be. "And the message."

She'd always heard turnabout was fair play.

Maybe the good she'd done for others was about to rub off on her.

"WHAT'S A GUY LIKE YOU doing in a swanky place like this?" asked a familiar voice over the blasting music of a dance set.

The hair along his neck raising, Blade Stone turned from the drink he was mixing to his newest customer at the Club Undercover bar. Behind her, a halo of red engulfed the dance floor and worked its way up the tiered seating. Blue neon from behind him washed over her features without dimming them. She was beaming at him, and despite the fact that several years had gone by since he'd last seen that face, he connected with her instantly.

"Star Jacobek, aren't you a sight."

Her eyebrows shot up. "I go by my given name now. Detective Star would sound a little…well, weird, huh?"

"So you made detective. I always knew you could do anything you set your mind to."

Raised in the same impoverished neighborhood on Chicago's South Side, they'd grown up together, friends who'd shared good times and bad. They'd been pursued by the same gang for initiation, but they'd hung together and resisted, a life of crime being an anathema to them both. As a matter of fact, they'd taken similar directions as adults, she with the police force, he with the military.

For him, that had been a lifetime ago, but for her it was an obvious current reality.

"So, you're Detective Stella Jacobek now." Though in his mind she would always be Star, the bright light who'd led him out of the darkness that had been his childhood. How could he have let that friendship slip away, no matter what had happened to him? And now she might be that bright light for him once more. "Well then, let's celebrate your promotion, Starshine."

"I'm off duty," she said brightly.

"I'll get you a beer," he said, remembering her preference. "Give me a minute."

Blade quickly finished mixing the drinks he'd been working on and set them on a tray for the waitress to pick up. Then he poured an imported beer for his old friend and a cola for himself.

"So why are you gunning for me out of the blue?" she asked, referring to the message he'd left for her.

"And how are you gonna help me with Evelyn Cross?"

Tension gripped him as he slapped that morning's newspaper down on the bar. Gazing out from the front page was a lovely if apprehensive woman who was supported on both sides by paramedics as they left a strip motel. The headline read Abducted Woman Rescued.

"Tell me about her," Blade demanded, though he already knew enough.

"Evelyn Cross is a divorce lawyer—a big shot who does a lot of pro bono. Remember Carla Rincon? She got Carla away from Johnny before he beat her to death."

Staring at the printed face, at the woman's frightened eyes especially, Blade felt more than his gut tighten. "And *you* saved *her?*"

She shook her head. "But I'm investigating. The guy who grabbed her is still out there, Blade. He threatened to kill her and she's ready to run. And with the budget cuts in the department—"

"How about I play bodyguard?"

Her expression held more than a touch of suspicion. "Why?"

"I have reasons. Personal."

"Interesting." Her suspicious expression softened, becoming curious. "Anything you can tell me?"

"I'll let you know." If he ever could talk about what he'd done, that was.

Thinking about it for a moment, she nodded. "All right, then. If you could give her a safe place for a few days, maybe she would stick around, so when we do find the offender, she can nail him."

"Define *safe.*"

"Away from her ivory tower. He knows where to find her. He called her tonight and made more threats. She didn't wait to start packing, but I made her promise to give me an hour to come up with a plan." Stella shrugged and made a face. "You're it?" she said hopefully.

A burst of surety swept through him. He'd needed absolution for what had seemed like forever—not that he could ever really make up for what he'd done—this was his shot.

The owner, Gideon, and a few other Club Undercover employees like Logan and Cassandra—Team Undercover, as they called themselves jokingly—would relish a chance to help another innocent. He didn't ever have to tell them why he'd chosen Evelyn Cross in particular.

So Blade nodded and raised his glass once more, and let his mouth soften to an unaccustomed smile. "I'm it."

THE LONGEST HOUR of her life was coming to an end.

Lynn paced the length of her living room and glanced at the clock. Again. Just as she had nearly every minute that ticked away.

Three minutes left.

"C'mon, Detective, call."

Because Lynn really didn't want to turn tail and run, didn't want to lose herself and become some nameless face in another city, she'd had her hopes pinned on the other woman. But she simply couldn't stay put and wait for the other shoe to drop.

He could be anywhere, waiting…watching.

He could be outside her apartment building right this very moment, ready to strike again!

The phone rang. Tony said, "Detective Jacobek to see you."

"Send her up, please."

A glance at the clock told her the detective had returned with a whole minute to spare.

Even so, a knock at the door a few minutes later nearly made her trip over her packed suitcase.

"Thank God!" Unlocking the door, she swung it wide, saying, "I didn't think you were going to make it."

"Here I am."

Her eyes widened at the sight of the dangerous-looking man whose dark hair framed equally dark eyes, broad cheekbones, a high-bridged nose and a mouth drawn into a thin, unsmiling line. Her heart thundered in her chest and took away her breath. Still hanging on to the metal panel, she tried shutting him out, but he was already in the doorway.

In? He filled it.

Her mind whirled as she backed up, wishing she had some kind of weapon to use against him.

"I'm here to—"

Interrupting, she said, "Get out now or—"

"Or what?" he asked quietly, still coming for her.

She could imagine that deep voice lowered to a whisper, taunting her, threatening her.

It had to be him—her abductor—but how had he gotten past security?

Wildly, she looked around for a weapon and settled on a piece of metal sculpture that had cost her a week's salary. Grabbing it, she brandished it wildly, pointing its sharp edges toward him.

"I wouldn't do that, if I were you," he warned. "It looks dangerous. You might hurt something."

"Yeah—you!"

She swung with all her might. When the heavy sculpture dragged her toward him, he ducked to one side. She lost her balance, whacked her hip into his and let the sculpture drop. It hit the back of his leg before bouncing to the floor.

He grunted and his dark eyes narrowed. "I told you that damn thing was dangerous."

"So am I!" she yelled, slashing at his face with her long nails.

He grabbed her wrist inches from his eyes and easily held it there, somehow without actually hurting her. "I think you have me confused with someone else. I'm—"

"A no-good wannabe murderer!"

In her struggle to free herself, a strap on her sandal broke and Lynn went flying backward. To her horror, she jerked him off balance and he flew with her. Her back smacked against the carpeted floor and she steeled herself for a heavy jolt that never came, for he threw out an arm and caught himself with another grunt.

Hand flat against the floor, he levered himself over her, in a one-armed push-up. Though he wasn't touching her, his heat seared her, gluing her to the spot. Then something fell from the opening of his shirt and brushed against her face, and she realized it was some kind of leather pouch hanging around his neck.

As to the man himself, he was far too close for comfort. Close enough that his eyes seemed black— so black she couldn't distinguish pupil from iris. Close enough to tell his hair was longer than it looked, merely pulled back and tied with leather at the nape of his neck. Close enough that she had to force herself not to move lest she touch any part of his incredibly well muscled body.

"I'm here to—"

"I know what you're here for," she said, shoving at his chest, to no avail. He was as immovable as a rock. "And you're not going to get it. Help!"

"Stop that!"

She only screamed louder.

He put a hand over her mouth. "Stop screaming and listen, will you?"

You're the one who does all the talking…

Wasn't that what her abductor had said to her right before she'd been rescued?

"All right, let's try again," he said in a voice nearly as soft as a whisper.

Terrified, Lynn couldn't move. Couldn't speak even if his hand weren't covering her mouth. He was going to try to kill her again, and this time there was no one to stop him.

She heard a sound from the hall, followed by a choked exclamation. "Blade Stone, I always heard you were a fast worker, but this must be a record, even for you."

Lynn darted her gaze beyond him to the doorway, where Detective Stella Jacobek leaned against the jamb.

Chapter Two

"If I let go of you and get up, can I trust you not to try to hurt me again?" Blade asked.

Lynn answered with another question. "Why didn't you tell me you were with Stella?"

"I tried. You wouldn't let me."

"I answered the door, expecting her, and find you standing there." She didn't know which was stronger, her anger or her embarrassment. "What am I supposed to think?"

"That's another thing. What are you doing answering the door if you don't know who's on the other side? Don't you have any sense?"

Lynn craned her neck, peering around him toward the detective, whose expression was more amused than concerned. "Who is this jerk?"

"Your new bodyguard."

"What?"

Blade pushed himself off of her. "I'm having second thoughts myself."

"You are not." Stella came forward and, stepping between them, played referee. "Lynn, you couldn't find a better man to protect you than Blade Stone here. You can trust him with your life."

"Blade? You want me to trust a man who calls himself Blade?"

"Yes. His real name's Richard. Blade's a nickname."

"What kind of man goes by the name of Blade?" Lynn muttered, righting her dropped sculpture.

"One who's expert with knives," he answered.

She took another step back, to put some breathing room between them. Lynn was finding it hard to breathe, anyway. This man would intimidate anyone. Which, she thought, probably made him the perfect bodyguard.

"So you what?" She tried to ignore him and connect with Stella. "Expect me to stay put and let him move in here with me?"

"No," Blade said, "you're coming with me."

Lynn whipped around to face him. She was supposed to let a man she didn't even know control her life? "Who says? Where?"

"We'll provide you with a safe place to stay, a new look, a new identity."

"We who?"

"Some people I work with."

"What kind of work do you do?"

"I'm the head bartender at a place called Club Undercover."

She made a sound of exasperation and set the sculpture back on its stand. "Maybe I can still catch a red-eye out to…well, anywhere."

"Don't jump to any conclusions about Blade here. If anyone knows how to protect you, he does."

The word "protect" gave Lynn an itch in places she couldn't start to scratch. "A bartender might be versatile enough to give a drunk the bum's rush, but—''

''The bartender gig is temporary,'' Blade said. ''Don't worry, I was trained to handle danger. I won't let anything happen to you. We got off on the wrong foot. How about we start over. I'm a long-time friend of Stella here, and I agreed to help her out by watching over you while she's busy with the investigation.''

A bodyguard…she supposed she needed one…and this guy appeared to be as fit as they came. As long as he didn't push too hard, she could stand it.

She asked Stella, ''You have no doubts about this?''

''I would trust Blade with my life.''

Sizing Blade up, Lynn said, ''You scared me and I overreacted. If you're willing to start fresh, then so am I. About your fee—''

''I have my own reasons for wanting to do this, and they don't include money.''

Lynn took a deep breath. She had to be able to count on someone, and if she couldn't trust the detective who would see to her case, then who?

Lynn held out her hand, and though she wasn't a small woman, she felt as though it was engulfed by his. When she glanced into his dark eyes, she was caught by something unfathomable. A connection of sorts. But of course, that was simply her imagination working overtime.

Suddenly uneasy, Lynn pulled her hand from his. ''All right then. Um, give me a minute. My strap broke—'' she indicated her disabled sandal ''—and I need to change into another pair.''

''Wear something sensible,'' Blade told her.

Lynn clenched her jaw. Oh, he liked being in control, all right. Before she could respond that she would wear what she liked—and she loved footwear that had nothing sensible about it—Stella cleared her throat.

"Can I leave now?" the detective asked. "Promise you won't try to kill each other?"

"Sounds like a safe bet." Remembering the tape with the message, Lynn handed it over and then backed off toward her bedroom. "And Stella, thanks for doing this."

The detective flashed Blade another strange look. Then she said, "I'm going to your office tomorrow, Lynn, to see if anyone has anything. In the meantime, you keep thinking about who might want to hurt you. You have my cell number and I have yours. What about you, Blade?"

"Not my choice of weapon."

Wondering if he'd actually made a joke, Lynn gave him a look of surprise, then limped toward her bedroom. "I'll be right back."

In addition to changing into slightly less delicate footwear, she took a comb to her hair, touched up her bruised cheek and swiped a pale peach gloss over her lips. Not that she was trying to impress the potential control-freak in the other room, she told herself. She simply had certain standards about her appearance, and she'd been too much in a dither earlier to make certain she was presentable.

But if Blade noticed when she emerged from the bedroom, she couldn't tell. He wore a passive expression, checked out her slightly more sensible sandals without comment and picked up her smaller bag and hung it over his shoulder.

"Ready?"

"As I'll ever be," she said, swallowing hard.

He swung the larger case up so easily it might have been empty, which it definitely was not. An hour gave a girl plenty of time to pack more than she needed.

"That thing has wheels," she pointed out.

"Uh-huh."

But he was already halfway out the door and didn't pause to make things easier for himself. That is, if the considerable weight of the suitcase bothered him at all, which it didn't seem to. Oh, he was so terribly macho...

Carrying nothing but her purse, Lynn followed him into the hallway and locked the door behind them, hoping it wouldn't be long before she could return to the only peaceful home she'd ever known.

Turning, she saw that her new bodyguard was already holding the elevator door open for her. If he was impatient, he didn't show it. Lynn took her time getting in the car. The hour was late and it seemed they were the only ones using the elevator, because the first stop was the lobby.

When they passed the security desk, Tony asked, "Going on another business trip so soon, Ms. Cross? Are you sure you're okay?"

"I'll be fine, Tony, and I'll see you in a few days."

"Have a good flight, then."

She didn't correct him, but headed after Blade, who now stood at the outside doors, waiting for her. Her bodyguard sure didn't wait around to watch her back.

Okay, so that wasn't fair. Being a bodyguard wasn't exactly his business. He was doing Stella—and her—a favor. So she needed an attitude adjustment. Surely she could get along with him for a few days. She might not be looking forward to spending time with Blade on his turf, but she certainly felt more comfortable leaving her building with him at her side than she would have alone.

"He could be out here," she murmured, moving closer.

"Not near enough to get to you."

"How do you know?"

"He'd have to go through me."

It was an answer that caused her to swallow, because he was dead serious. Instinct told her that he was aware of every sound, every movement, every life-form within sight or hearing. As if he were trained to do so, she thought, but how might he have gotten that particular training? He probably wouldn't appreciate her questioning him.

Besides, Stella had insisted she could trust him, and so trust him Lynn would.

Guilt washed through her when she noticed Blade was limping a little, undoubtedly a result of her whacking him with the sculpture. Either he was too preoccupied to notice, or he was ignoring the hurt.

He stopped at the only vehicle parked in front of her building—illegally, but lucky for him, he hadn't gotten a ticket—and she wondered what use he got out of a Jeep in the city. He wasn't the yuppie type. More of a back-to-nature kind of guy, if the jeans and boots and soft brown shirt open at the throat, sleeves rolled up to reveal arms roped with muscle, were any indication. Could that be how he'd honed his instincts, his expertise with a knife? By hunting?

He stashed her luggage in the back, opened the passenger door and offered her a hand.

Ignoring it, she said, "Thanks," and slipped inside. Once they were on their way, and had crossed

North Michigan Avenue and were traveling through the trendy River North area, which even at this hour was still crowded with suburbanites and tourists, Lynn picked a safer subject than what had been rattling through her head. "So tell me about this Club Undercover."

"It's a late night dance club, and what goes on earlier in the evening varies from night to night. Poetry slams, performance art—you name it. Audiences seem to enjoy the variety."

It sounded frenetic to her, but she wasn't about to spend any more time in the club than necessary. "Personally, I find a night at the ballet or the opera or an opening at a gallery enjoyable."

"Ah, snob stuff."

"I'm no snob. We just…move in different circles."

"You can say that again."

She gave him an intense look. Did he mean to sound superior? If he did, he wasn't gloating, merely concentrating on driving and checking the rearview mirror.

For a moment, Lynn was mesmerized by his profile, the high-bridged nose, especially. This, added to his eyes, revealed perhaps Native American ancestry, maybe the reason he seemed so dark and dangerous.

Her breath catching, she said, "You mentioned changing my identity. Have you done this before?"

He gave her a quick glance. "Is that the officer of the court speaking?"

"Try the worried victim."

Stopping at a light, Blade turned to face her more fully. "Once, for a woman wrongly incarcerated."

"What have you got going—some kind of covert operation?" she asked.

"Uh, nothing you have to worry about. Except to keep it to yourself."

"Okay, I'm not in any position to give you a hard time. Your secret dies with me," she joked, making a cross over her heart. "So, does anyone have any ideas about how to approach this investigation?"

"Whoa. Who said anything about our investigating?" The light changed and they were off again, still heading west. "I simply volunteered to keep you safe. That's it."

Lynn tried to pretend she wasn't disappointed, but she couldn't lie to herself. For a brief moment, she'd thought she could be more than a victim in hiding, that with the proper help she might figure her own way out of this mess. After all, who knew her own life better than she? Of course a little recall of the actual event might help, but so far, she had nothing on that score. Not that she'd had time to pursue it.

"So where do you plan to stash me?"

"In plain sight. You're in luck. We just lost a waitress, and Gideon said you can replace her."

"Lucky me?" Lynn was aghast at the prospect of waiting tables, something she'd never done, not even while in school. "I'm a lawyer, for heaven's sake!"

"If you're on the lam you're not going to be practicing law now, are you?"

She hadn't given the question due consideration. She would have to call her firm and tell them she was taking a leave of absence for an undetermined time. Still…

"I don't need to work for tips. I have enough money to pay my way."

"So how are you going to blend in? Sitting at the bar alone every night, all night, watching me fill drink orders? A woman like you will be bored. And noticeable."

They'd left the populated area and were heading up a deserted street—part of the old manufacturing corridor. Filled with growing trepidation fed by their lonely surroundings, Lynn said, "I wasn't planning on spending any more time at the club than I have to."

"Well, I'm not planning on quitting my job," he informed her quietly. "If you want my help, you'll have to compromise your standards a little."

He was applying the snob factor to her again!

Lynn sank into silence and seethed for the rest of the drive through an impoverished neighborhood whose streets were equally deserted. There was no use arguing with Blade, no matter that his telling her what to do was like nails on a chalkboard. She'd had enough of that growing up. Her father had ruled their home by intimidation and denigration, and had made anyone who defied him sorry.

So she would go along with Blade's plan for the moment—until she figured out a better one of her own.

ONCE CALLED the Polish Gold Coast, Wicker Park and the adjoining Bucktown neighborhood were now home to an eclectic mix of residents. Artists had moved in when space was affordable, while city housing had been made available to the less fortunate. And then young professionals had been drawn by the proximity to the downtown area, and gentrification had begun.

The Chicago skyline sparkled with lights in the distance as Blade guided Lynn along Milwaukee Avenue toward the building with a fancy tile facade that housed Club Undercover. A cacophony of sound assaulted his ears the moment they neared the cavelike entrance to the below-street-level club. Patrons in their twenties and thirties were bouncing up and down the wide stairway, somehow having conversations with their companions despite the competing thump-thump of bass coming from the sound system below.

"How can anyone have a conversation over all this noise?" Lynn asked, raising her voice a few decibels above the blasting music.

Blade arched his eyebrows. "What noise?" He was used to it.

She rolled her eyes and dodged a guy with brilliant green hair who was walking up the stairs backward.

Lynn would get used to it all, too, Blade thought.

"Hang on a second."

He approached the hostess, Mags, whose current dark orange hair matched her skimpy garment, which looked more like a long tube top than a dress.

"Would you ask Cassandra and Logan to meet me in Gideon's office?"

"Sure thing, Blade."

Wearing headsets with a mike attached, as did all the wait staff, she relayed the message. Lynn was staring into the club itself, lit in neon blue and red, the floor packed with frantic dancers gyrating to Nebula's "Come Down." The club was a two-story affair, and the seating area rose in tiers, the highest being at street level.

Blade turned his charge from the entryway toward a quieter hallway.

His calf was burning where she'd clobbered him with that sculpture, and he was trying not to show it. His plan was to ice the bruised area when he got back to his place. In the meantime, he focused on the sensation and mentally dissipated the pain as he'd been trained to do.

Lynn had been awfully silent after their discussion about her spending time at the club that was now like home to him. He wondered what she was thinking. Being a lawyer, she was probably planning some kind of strategy. He could see he had his work cut out for him.

As long as she didn't plan another physical attack, he thought, biting back a smile. He had to give her points for that one. Though she sure had guts, he didn't think she was as tough as she pretended to be. Those eyes, up close a stormy gray, were a dead giveaway. He wondered how she ever bluffed an opponent in a legal standoff.

Then again, not everyone read people as easily as he did.

"In here."

He leaned over to grasp the doorknob, and got a closer whiff of her exotic scent, a bit of pungent spice mixed with a subtle floral fragrance. He'd smelled it when they'd hit the floor together, so close that... well, he'd been hard-pressed to remain professional. The perfume and the strappy sandals were certainly interesting choices for the woman hiding in lawyer's clothing.

Cass would fix the rest, Blade thought, letting a smile settle on his lips as he led Lynn into his boss's inner sanctum.

LYNN SHORTLY FOUND HERSELF surrounded by testosterone—club owner Gideon at his desk, Blade next to her and security expert John Logan to the rear.

With its black-and-chrome furniture, and walls the same deep blue as the owner's eyes, the office was as masculine as the man himself. Gideon wore his longish, blue-black hair slicked away from classically handsome features that could easily grace the cover of a men's magazine.

Suddenly an equally striking woman burst through the doorway, demanding, "Did I miss anything? I was in the middle of setting up my next illusion." To Lynn, she explained, "I do a little magic for the customers between sets."

"The Amazing Cassandra is very versatile," Gideon agreed, then said, "We were just making introductions. Our new client, Evelyn Cross...Cassandra Freed."

"Client?" Lynn murmured, Gideon's inflection making her wonder what she'd gotten herself into.

"Gideon can be a little intimidating," Cass said, shaking Lynn's hand, "but he's got a soft heart."

Lynn liked the other woman right away. Her smile lit up an interesting face surrounded by a long mass of mahogany hair tipped with brilliant fuchsia the same shade as her short dress and long nails.

"So what's the plan?" Logan asked, still leaning against the back wall. He flicked an invisible speck of dust from the lapel of his designer suit jacket. Good-looking in his own way, he had rugged features topped by silver-threaded light brown hair spiked in a contemporary buzz cut.

"Simple," Blade said. "We give Lynn a new look, some new ID and protection. I'll take care of the last."

Startled by his possessive tone, Lynn gave him a wide-eyed stare and wondered if three such seemingly potent men were able to work together smoothly. The male lawyers at her firm were always trying to find ways to one-up each other, and they were wimps compared to these guys.

"I can give you a full makeover tomorrow," Cass stated. "Any preference for hairstyle or color? Oh, never mind. We can figure it out in the morning. My place. Not too early," she warned Blade.

"Yes, ma'am," he said.

Cassandra's style really wasn't her own, Lynn thought. "Wouldn't some makeup and a new outfit—"

Gideon ran right over her halfhearted protest. "We just want you to be safe, to make sure no one recognizes you. If you have a name you'd prefer to use, let me know."

Lynn's heart drummed in her throat, making it difficult for her to speak. They were taking over her life, and they were doing it by being organized in techniques that could be used to scam others. The officer of the court in her went on alert, but the victim gladly turned off the radar. Besides, she could use any name she wanted as long as it wasn't to commit a crime. For once she would voluntarily give up control of her life.

Gideon cleared his throat. "The only thing we ask of you in return is that you keep quiet about the help we're giving you."

"Blade already clued me in."

"Then you're agreed?"

"Agreed. I'm in your hands," she said, hoping she wouldn't live to regret those words.

Chapter Three

"So where are you going to put me up?" Lynn asked Blade once they were on their way again in the Jeep.

"It's only a few blocks from here. There's a vacancy next door to me, and I'll contact the landlord in the morning, so for tonight it'll be my place."

"Excuse me?"

"I have a nice big bed. Very comfortable."

She imagined it was, but the very thought of sharing it with him made her decidedly uncomfortable. "Well, *I'm* not sleeping in your bed."

"Then you can have the couch and I'll take the bed."

He'd been planning on sleeping on the couch and giving her the bed? The heat of embarrassment at her assumption crawled up her neck. Why hadn't he just said so? Now she was stuck with the arrangement.

Unless…

"Any hotels around here?"

"It would be difficult to keep tabs on you if you were bunking in a hotel, Lynn."

"We could get adjoining rooms. On me, of course."

"We'll *be* in adjoining rooms. Well, sort of."

Whatever that meant.

Lynn bit back further argument. Blade Stone owed her nothing; he was simply baby-sitting her as a favor to Detective Jacobek. Lynn couldn't make him go even further out of his way than he already had.

Though she didn't have to like it, she would take the couch, which really was only fair. After all, they were going to his place, where she would be the intruder, albeit an invited one. Besides, there was a lot more of him than her. He probably didn't even fit on the couch.

A speculation that activated her imagination.

For a moment, she saw him in her mind's eye, sprawled over the bed...naked. His muscular body would be beautiful, all bronzed angles and planes...

Flushing, she forced the image away. They had nothing in common, so she shouldn't be indulging in such whimsy. Besides, whimsy wasn't appropriate in her situation. She needed to concentrate on the issue at hand—her continued safety.

"So where did you get your training?" she asked as he turned the Jeep into an alley.

"Mixing drinks?"

"Bodyguarding," she said.

He pulled into a diagonal spot behind a three-story building. "You're my first."

No experience. Oh, great! Hopefully the sheer size of him would make most men think twice about crossing him. Besides, she needed to trust the detective's judgment.

So she said, "Okay, weapons."

"Which ones?"

"Let's start with knives." The source of his nickname.

His answer—"On the mean streets of Chicago"—
didn't surprise her.

He cut the engine and they left the Jeep. Blade
pulled her luggage out of the back and hefted it as
easily as he had earlier.

"We'll go up the back way."

Lynn followed him down the walkway to the open
stairwell and noticed that he was still limping. Actually, the hitch looked more pronounced than it had
earlier, which meant he must really be hurting.

Frowning, wondering why he hadn't said anything
or done anything about it, she kept her own counsel.
Instead, she circled back to their conversation. "So,
you were part of a gang growing up?"

"I fought to stay out of one."

"And then did what?"

"Joined the military."

Which meant he knew how to handle not only himself but weapons far scarier than knives. "Did you go
overseas?"

"A few times."

"You weren't stationed there?"

"Not for any length of time."

"Then for what?"

"Special…assignments."

"Could you be more cryptic?"

"I could try if you really want me to."

Though she would swear that was his attempt at
humor, she didn't think he was really joking with her.
Just giving her the runaround.

She guessed he must be a private person. And she,
being a lawyer, was too nosey for many people. Obviously for him, as well. Another example of how

they were oil and water. She wanted to know everything. He wanted to tell nothing.

He started up the back stairs and she could see he was having some trouble climbing.

"Give me that suitcase," she said, reaching for it.

Blade didn't let go and the result was her drawing up close and personal. The heat of his arm seared Lynn so badly that she froze and considered letting him have the damn case.

And then she changed her mind.

Through gritted teeth, she insisted, "I can handle my own bag."

He shrugged and let go, and the weight almost pushed her back down the stairs. Quickly recovering, she carefully balanced the suitcase and pulled the handle out of the back before turning it around.

"Anyone with any sense would do it the easy way," she informed him.

"I don't know. For some women, the harder the better."

With that, he turned away from her and more easily took the stairs, leaving her suspicious once more about his verbal intent. Surely she wasn't crazy—he was trying to get a rise out of her, wasn't he? So why didn't that surprise her? Who better than she would know a man wanted to have the upper hand over a woman?

One way or another.

Grunting as she bumped the heavy wheeled case up one step at a time—all the way to the third floor—she decided not to let his low-key humor get to her. And by the time she reached his landing and waited for him to unlock the back door, she was breathing hard.

While the back porches below had been barren, this one had a couple of resin chairs with a small table between them, a large house plant in one corner and another two flowering plants hanging from two sides of the porch roof. *Inviting,* she thought. Unlike the man himself.

"Who's your decorator?" she asked, wondering if a woman was involved, and how that other woman would like Lynn's bunking in with her boyfriend, even if only for tonight.

"The furniture's mine. The plants are compliments of my mother."

Mother, huh? Somehow Lynn hadn't imagined that.

A few more large hanging plants softened the nearly bare interior of what she quickly gathered was a single large room with an alcove off the kitchen, where she got a glimpse of his rumpled bed. When she'd mentioned adjacent rooms, he'd said that's what they'd have here. *Sort of.*

She got it. No privacy. Great. So she would sleep in her clothes.

But would he?

When he set her bag down between the couch and the single upholstered chair, she said, "Your leg... How is it?"

"I'll live."

"But you've been limping. Maybe you should have it checked out."

"I'd prefer icing it. You could use some ice on those wrists, as well."

Lynn looked down at the bruises and scrapes where the ropes had bound her. "No, I'm fine."

"If you say so." He started for the kitchen. "Can I get you something to drink? I have beer and cola."

"You wouldn't have tea?" Which would soothe her raw throat.

"I do if you'll drink herbal."

"Perfect."

What kind of man served herbal tea? she wondered. And had house plants and flowers on his back porch? Blade Stone certainly was unusual.

Lynn watched him move around the tiny kitchen area, putting mugs filled with water in the microwave and fetching a tray of ice cubes from the freezer and emptying them into a plastic bag. He was at ease, undoubtedly the same way he would be behind the bar when he was serving up drinks at the club.

Blade Stone, a bartender. She couldn't help but wonder why he would settle for a dead-end job when surely the military had trained him for something more challenging. Then again, bartending in a fast-paced, upscale club might pay better. And maybe she was too demanding, not only of herself, but of others, as well.

Joining her, he set two mugs down on the coffee table.

"No tea bags?"

"Special brew. Let it settle for a few minutes and it'll be fine."

"Special how?"

He set the bag of ice on the coffee table and gingerly laid his leg on it. "Guaranteed to calm you down and let you get a good night's sleep."

Skeptical, she wondered if she would sleep at all, what with all the thoughts about who and why roiling through her mind. She'd put her fears on hold for a while, maybe because of Blade, but the reminder prompted a resurfacing of anxiety.

"Don't worry, I won't let him get to you," he said, his tone low and soothing.

"How—"

"Your eyes. If you don't want people to know what you're thinking, you need to learn to hide it better."

"I thought I was pretty good at hiding things."

"As in?"

She shook her head. She didn't want to talk about it. He was nearly a stranger, for heaven's sake, and she had no desire to relate her life's story to him or anyone else, for that matter.

Eager to change the subject, she asked, "How's the leg?"

He made a face and shrugged. "It's getting numb."

"I think someone should take a look at it."

"You?"

She blinked and said, "I guess."

"So you're not sure if you want to look at my leg."

He was playing word games with her again. "I meant I'm no expert. But I can't see anything unless you roll up your jeans."

Lowering his foot, he tried to do so. "Won't go high enough."

"Then you'll have to take them off."

"If you insist." He rose and unbuckled his belt.

"Whoa. That's not what I meant."

He gave her a knowing grin. "Don't worry, I can take care of it."

He limped across the room, opened the door to the bathroom and started making rustling noises. And then she heard a low curse that made her wince.

Lynn couldn't stop herself from investigating. Just one peek, she thought, getting up from the couch and crossing to the door, which was still open a crack. What she saw made her gasp and swing the door wide.

"You've been bleeding!"

Though the blood had dried, it covered most of his calf, and he was standing on his good leg trying to tend to it. Never mind that he wasn't wearing any pants. Never mind that a leather sheath holding a knife was strapped to his other calf.

Never having thought herself capable of violence, she was truly appalled when she said, "I can't believe I actually wounded you."

BLADE STARED at the lovely woman who'd gone pale at the sight of his dried blood and looked ready to faint. Wonderful.

"It's just a scratch. Honest." Though it hurt like hell.

"Sit and I'll take care of it."

"I told you that sculpture was dangerous."

She glanced at the antiseptic on the sink. "Where's your first aid kit?"

He tilted his head. "That would be it."

Lynn pushed at his chest until he sat on the throne. Then she filled the sink with hot water, found his meager stack of linens and threw a washcloth into the bowl. It seemed she wasn't going to pass out on him, after all.

He watched in fascination as she knelt before him and gently cleaned his wound. Her fingers were light on his flesh, but trembling.

For a moment, he thought about other, more intimate things she could do for him while down there on her knees. Thankfully, his shirttails were long

enough to hide his briefs and the erection that flared
to life within them.

"It's more than a scratch," Lynn said, her gentle
touch continuing to cause him discomfort. "But it did
stop bleeding on its own, so I guess you don't need
stitches. You do have some kind of bandages, right?"

Blade pointed up to the medicine cabinet and was
mesmerized as she stood and reached over him toward the cabinet, her breasts nearly brushing his face
in the process. He swallowed hard and fought back
the urge to do something about the physical stirrings
plaguing him.

"All right," she murmured, bringing down the box
with something akin to an expression of victory. Back
down on her knees before him, she opened the pack-
aging of a large strip bandage. "So why didn't you
say anything about being cut?"

"I had other things on my mind."

As he did now. Inappropriate things. Things he
wanted her to do with those hands that were driving
him crazy. Using the same technique he had earlier
against the pain, he steeled himself against her.

"Getting me away from my building so fast wasn't
that urgent," she said, looking up at him.

Lynn's eyes were clear, innocent of the heat she'd
inspired in him.

"On the other hand," he said, "you gave us the
definite impression that you were ready to fly away
immediately."

"But I'm not heartless, and I was responsible for
hurting you." Frowning, she concentrated on attach-
ing the bandage. "And you passed up a second opportunity at the club."

"By then I had the pain under control."

"How?"

"A technique I was taught in the military." Admitting it was no breach of confidentiality. "Just in case."

"Just in case *what?*"

"In case we were ever caught and tortured."

As if she found that unbelievable, she shook her head and muttered, "Men. No matter what happens, you have to be in control."

"And you don't?"

"Not in the same way, no." She applied a second bandage. "But I don't want someone controlling me, either."

"That was obvious." He clarified, saying, "The suitcase."

"Done." She closed the box and got to her feet. "Now you should take advantage of that ice before it's nothing but a puddle. And I'm going to go get that tea."

Lynn left him alone in the bathroom. Watching her go, his eyes settling on her lush derriere, Blade acknowledged the desire that taunted him despite his resolve. She was some woman.

Too bad her last name was Cross.

Climbing back into his jeans, he adjusted himself and zipped them up before following her into the main room. She was already curled into one corner of the couch and sipping her tea.

"Mmm. Good," she said.

As if the herbs were already working their magic on her, she seemed more relaxed. Or maybe it was simply because she felt safer than she had earlier.

Deciding to play it safe himself, he took the chair opposite her. No need to tempt fate.

He settled his leg back up on the ice packet and took a slug of the special brew he'd concocted long ago when he himself had been desperate to sleep. He knew the healing ability of the herbs would let her drift away from the horror of what had happened to her. Still, before she did, he needed some details.

Watching her carefully, he said, "So tell me about the abduction."

Her fingers immediately tensed on her mug. "There's not much I *can* tell you. I was working late. He got me as I was coming out of the building. I never saw him. He used drugs. A blindfold. Intimidation."

"Do you think it was someone you know?"

"It must be. A client's ex-spouse most likely. I remember him telling me to think about what I'd done."

"You didn't recognize the voice?"

She shook her head. "He never spoke in a normal tone. I never knew how chilling a whisper could be."

Lynn shivered and her eyes went all dark and stormy again. And Blade wanted in the worst way to take back the question that so disturbed her, to reach out and engulf her in his arms, to reassure her that he would protect her with his own life if necessary.

Sacrificing his life for hers, after all, would only be fair.

LYNN HAD TO ADMIT the herbal tea did its job. She was soon yawning and fighting to keep her eyes open.

"Bedtime," she murmured, following that with a big yawn. "Do you have an extra pillow?"

"Why don't you just take the bed."

The bed with rumpled sheets that probably smelled all male and inviting, like him, she thought.

"Uh-uh. I have dibs on the couch."

"If you're sure."

She scooted down and got comfortable. Maybe she didn't need a pillow. She was already drifting....

Aware of a strong hand cupping her head and lifting it, she felt her head settle on something soft and cool and comforting. A pillow.

"Thanks," she murmured, then felt the light weight of a sheet cover her body as her mind drifted toward darkness....

You're the one who does all the talking.

Startled, she sat straight up in a darkened room, untangling her limbs from the sheet, her heart pounding. The voice... Whose was it?

Though she strained to hear, she caught no further sound. Still, danger lurked somewhere nearby.

She had to get out of there.

"Blade!" she whispered sharply, and when he didn't answer, she panicked and got to her feet, sensing more than seeing her way to the front door, which she fought open.

Once through the doorway, she was caught. Arms like ropes surrounded her, and she couldn't even fight back.

She screamed once before a cruel hand forced a cloth over her mouth and jerked back her neck so that her head clunked against something hard. Something that cracked. And then a foul scent filled her senses and her head began to whirl even as she struggled to free herself once more....

"Lynn, wake up."

Blade's voice. His hand was shaking her shoulder, rocking her up out of the depths of a nightmare.

With a gasp, she opened her eyes and saw Blade hunkered down next to the couch. Not thinking, she cried out and threw her arms around his neck, hanging on for dear life.

"It's all right," he murmured soothingly. "Everything is going to be all right."

"I thought…I thought he had me again."

"A bad dream. You're here with me. You're safe."

"No, I'm not. I won't be safe until he's where he belongs—behind bars."

She was trembling with fear and anger, and Blade's attempt to comfort her with soothing strokes along her spine was doing something else entirely. Her body was awakening to his touch, telling her that she was alive.

Alive…but for how long?

Until we meet again…

Who knew how long it would be before that happened? What if her abductor had the means to find her no matter where she hid?

Then what?

Desperate for reassurance, she wrapped her arms tighter around Blade and realized that the only thing he seemed to be wearing was the leather pouch hanging from his neck. His flesh had a life of its own beneath her hands. Her palms tingled and her fingers wouldn't be still. They kneaded his back and climbed higher until they tangled in his long hair, now freed from the leather that had bound it earlier.

Stiffening, he protested, "Uh, Lynn, maybe—"

"Shh," she whispered, her lips now nuzzling his

ear. "Please. You make me feel alive. Don't stop letting me feel like I'm alive."

With a groan, he swept his fingers through her hair. She turned her face to his and their mouths brushed and her lips began to tingle.

"More," she murmured, angling her head so that she could kiss him more fully.

His mouth covered hers and she opened to him, and when their tongues met, he moaned and captured her in a deep, wet, electrifying kiss. Her body was urgently assuring her that she was very much alive. Her toes were curling and her nipples hardening, and the sweet spot between her thighs was throbbing for his touch.

But even as he kissed her, he made no move to go further, so she slipped a hand down his back and around his waist and smiled into his mouth when his flesh quivered under her touch. And then she hit flesh that wasn't smooth, an area that felt taut. Damaged.

Scar tissue?

Not wanting to think about how he might have been wounded, she plunged her hand down his front to find him hot and hard and ready for exactly what she needed at this moment.

"Lynn—"

"Undress me," she whispered. "I want to feel your hands on me, touching me the way I'm touching you." She grasped him, slipping her circled fingers up to his tip. "I want to feel your mouth on me. I want you inside me, giving me your life force. I want to celebrate being alive."

For a moment, Lynn thought she had him convinced. He certainly felt alive against her hand. But then he pulled back and kept her from following, holding her at arm's length.

"Why not?"

"Because it's wrong."

"Don't worry," she said, her breath heavy, her womanly flesh slicked with a dampness she couldn't ignore. "I'll still be able to look at myself in the mirror tomorrow."

"The trouble is...I wouldn't be able to look at me."

Blade's words were like a dash of cold water, and Lynn snapped out of the trancelike state. He was right, of course. She was merely trying to use him.

Unfortunately, he wasn't going to let her use sex to get her through the night.

HE WAITED UNTIL THE NIGHT was still except for the lap of water against the riverbank. Until, as he could see through his binoculars, the security guard had taken to dozing in fits and starts.

Pulling on thin leather gloves, he went in the back way, the delivery entrance off the loading dock. After jamming the lock earlier, he'd kept watch. No one had been by since to notice.

As he took the fire stairs two at a time up to the lobby level, he went over his plan in his mind. No more slipups. This time he would get her where she lived, and his final victory over her would be all the sweeter. This time he wouldn't give her a chance to scream, to alert some busybody who would call the cops.

The sharp click of the lobby door startled him, but apparently not so the guard, who continued to doze with a soft snore.

Prepared for what he had to do, he slid silently forward and coldcocked the man before he could so much as stir. Then he quickly dragged the guard's limp body into the staff room. There he trussed him like a calf for branding and used duct tape to keep his trap shut so he couldn't scream for help. Grabbing the guard's keys, he left the man there for his morning relief to find.

Morning would be too late for Evelyn Cross.

He chuckled to himself as he imagined her shock when she realized she wasn't even safe in her own bed, after all.

But his grin died when the elevator door opened and he came face-to-face with a tall, sandy-haired guy in his early thirties. Ducking his head so that his billed cap would hide his face, he shoved past the guy without a word, then realized the man had turned to stare at him for a moment before heading for the guard's desk.

Damn, what if the prick could finger him?

"Hey, Tony, I'm leaving," the guy said even as the elevator doors closed.

Sweating now, not knowing what the other man would do when he realized the security guard wasn't behind his desk, he hit thirty-one, just in case. He didn't want anyone putting it together too soon.

The ride up took forever, the walk down three flights to twenty-eight longer.

He waited at the hallway fire door and listened. No sounds. If anyone was alerted, they wouldn't know where to look for him. And if he had the slightest worry about someone being on his tail, this was a damn big building. He could lose himself for as long as it took.

By the time he arrived at her door, he had the pass-key in hand. Listening hard, he heard nothing.

He was inside in a minute.

The room was dark, just as it ought to be, except for the moonlight streaming through the wall of windows. Enough light for him to see by. Enough to make out her bedroom door, which stood open.

This was all so easy it gave him a hard-on. Not that he would waste it on her. But it felt good. Made him feel powerful. He stroked himself through his trousers in anticipation as he slid into her bedroom, which was also illuminated by moonlight. The hard-on faded fast when he realized the bed was empty and still made.

Switching on a bedside lamp, he saw half-open drawers and a discarded outfit on a chair.

"Bitch!"

She'd gotten away.

But that was impossible! Through binoculars, he'd watched the woman detective escort her in the door and then leave some time later. And he'd waited to make certain Little Miss Goody Two-shoes didn't leave the building, as well.

Apparently he hadn't waited long enough.

A temporary setback.

If he didn't get her here, he would get her elsewhere, he told himself. Looking around and spotting her desk, he figured out how he could salvage the night's work.

It was merely a matter of time and then Evelyn Cross would be his to do with as he would.

Chapter Four

The next morning, Lynn couldn't look at Blade, but she wasn't sure if it was because they'd gone as far as they had or because he hadn't let it go further. He'd certainly kept control of the situation.

She took a long shower. After spending as much time as she could in the bathroom, she reluctantly opened the door. The odor of fresh coffee and cooked bacon wafted to her and her stomach protested.

"Breakfast is almost ready," he told her.

She mumbled, "I'm not a morning person."

"Consider it brunch."

If she ate with him she wouldn't be able to avoid looking at him, wouldn't be able to avoid the condemnation in his gaze. Still…not having had dinner the night before, she was starving.

"I guess I could eat a little something."

She glanced into the kitchenette. Fully dressed, his hair tied back from his face as it had been the day before, he was taking scrambled eggs out of the microwave. He split them between two dishes and then carried them into the main room, over to a small table against the wall opposite the couch.

Great. An intimate table for two. How lucky could she get?

"Help yourself to coffee."

She filled a mug and joined him at the table, where she stared at the food on her plate rather than at him. He'd wedged the eggs and bacon between two slices of toast.

"Mmm, a breakfast sandwich. Looks good." Taking a bite, she wasn't disappointed.

"It's easy. Easy is the only thing I can do with a microwave and hot plate. Eat up. Cassandra is bound to be awake by now."

Remembering her projected makeover, Lynn winced and swallowed. "You know, Cassandra looks really great, but she has her own style." Lynn dared to look Blade in the eye. "I'm not sure I'm up to being made over her by her."

"Don't worry," he said, as she took another bite, "she can hold herself back...unless you *want* purple hair."

Lynn nearly choked on her mouthful of food and then realized Blade was trying to cover up a smile. What in the world was she in for?

Deciding she'd be better able to handle the situation after eating, she chowed down. And gradually realized she felt more comfortable than she'd expected with the man. He hadn't referred to her middle-of-the-night gaffe. He hadn't so much as looked at her cross-eyed. So maybe she could continue to meet him eye-to-eye without cringing, after all.

She'd just finished her sandwich and was taking the last sip of coffee when he said, "That nightmare last night—do you remember it?"

Lynn's mouth went dry and she gripped her mug

tightly. "It was like I was being snatched all over again, only in this dark, nebulous hole."

"Maybe your mind was working on the problem while you slept. Your not being able to remember, that is."

"Like I was replaying what really happened. Right," she agreed. "But the episode was short. I thought I woke up and called for you, and then suddenly I knew he was there. I tried to get away, but I only got as far as the door before he snatched me and put this foul smelling rag over my face."

"So what about when you left your office building the other night?"

Concentrating, she could see the deserted street in her mind's eye, could remember wondering if she could even get a taxi that time of night. She remembered other things, as well, as replayed in her sleep.

She nodded. "That's what happened. Just like in my nightmare, he came from behind and covered my mouth and nose with a cloth."

"Do you remember anything else? Any details?"

Closing her eyes, Lynn replayed the scene in her head. "I tried struggling." Then she opened her eyes and met his gaze. "I whipped my head back and hit something hard."

"*His* head?"

"No. Something more than his head. I remember hearing a crack…like the sound of plastic breaking."

"Could he have been wearing a mask?"

Lynn struggled with the memory, but it would go no further. "I—I really don't know. But I don't think so." Concentrating, she could almost feel the impact again. "Whatever I hit had some kind of edge…like the corner of a pair of glasses. That's got to be it—I hit my head against his glasses and must have broken them.'' She shook her head. ''Not a great deal to go on.''

''But it's a detail you didn't have yesterday. It's a start.''

''Not enough to excite your detective friend.''

Blade didn't argue with her, merely said, ''The little things add up.''

''Well, then let's hope I remember lots of little details.''

''Don't pressure yourself and they'll come to you.''

Considering she'd been drugged through the experience, Lynn somehow doubted she would remember enough to count. She was getting a headache just thinking about it.

Blade stood and started clearing the table.

''Let me do that,'' she said.

''No big deal. Maybe there's someone you need to call? Phone's over there,'' he said, pointing to the wall near the bed.

''I'd better check in with work, give them a heads up that I'm taking a few days off to recover. And I'd better figure out what to tell my folks.''

''What about friends?''

''My two best friends are on vacation in Hawaii. I doubt they've heard a thing. They asked me to go with them. Too bad I didn't make the time.''

''Whatever you do, don't tell anyone where you are. Not here, not the club.''

''What? You think the man who abducted me is going to go to my parents or my office and ask where I am, and they'll just tell him?''

''Better not leave a trail or you might find a hungry wolf at your door.''

"Is that some old Indian saying or something?"

"That's common sense talking."

"Fine. I'll play I Spy."

As she made the calls, Lynn realized that she hadn't felt uncomfortable with Blade since she'd sat down to the table. He had an undeniable way of putting her at ease.

An hour later, when he delivered her to Cassandra's place a few blocks away—another third floor apartment, albeit more spacious—Lynn was actually nervous that he was going to leave and come back for both of them later, in time for work. Part of her wished he would stick around.

She followed Cass from the small foyer through a sparsely decorated living room and into an equally large room probably meant for dining. But Lynn noted a makeup table by the windows and a portable ballet bar along the opposite wall. And then there was the rack of colorful props on the way to the small kitchen. Show business stuff, she thought, remembering Gideon had called her the Amazing Cassandra.

"Blade won't even know you when I'm through with you," Cass said, indicating a chair. "Heck, your own mother won't know you."

"Um, that's what I'm afraid of," Lynn said, trying not to hurt the generous woman's feelings. "I appreciate your helping me and everything, but…what exactly did you have in mind?"

"Wow, you're even more conservative than I envisioned."

"I do have a life to go back to and soon. At least I hope so."

"You will. Our last case ended happily," Cass assured her.

"Last...the woman wrongly incarcerated that Blade told me about?"

"Right. She was wrongly convicted of murder and we—"

"Whoa! Murder? You don't mean the Mitchell woman?" The story had been in the paper for weeks.

"Elise Mitchell. I knew her a while back," Cass said evasively. "I made her into a whole new person. One look and Logan was in love. He and Elise have been an item ever since."

Lynn remembered reading that an ex-Detective John Logan had quit his job with the CPD to nail his sister's murderer himself. What she hadn't read was that he was connected to Club Undercover. The knowledge that the security chief was a former cop made Lynn feel a little better.

"Can we get started now?" Cass asked.

"Okay. Just keep in mind that I'm a lawyer with a serious reputation."

"One that I can ruin in a matter of minutes." Cass paused for a moment before saying, "Lynn, that was a joke. You can laugh now."

The best Lynn could come up with was a hopeful grimace. And then she asked, "What do you mean, envisioned?" Had Blade been telling Cass about her? When had he had the time?

"I sort of...have these hunches about people."

Lynn did laugh at that. "You mean you're psychic?"

"I don't like to label myself. I just know things other people don't."

Cass *was* claiming to be psychic, Lynn thought. "So what is it you know about me?"

"That you're a good person. That you've been disappointed by life. That you're not as together as you like to think.''

Generalities. Lynn smiled again. ''Millions of people could fit that profile.''

''True. And at least thousands have lost a loved one in the last couple of years. But they don't all blame themselves.''

Lynn started. How had Cass known that?

Not wanting to take the discussion further, Lynn asked, ''So what first?''

''Your hair, of course,'' she said, fingering the long, blond strands.

Two hours later, Lynn had to admit Cass knew what she was doing. The chin-length style with ragged edges would be easy enough to tame with another haircut when the charade was over. But Lynn thought the flattering silver-blond shade might have to stay.

''I look like a Kelly Ripa wannabe,'' she murmured, thinking of the talk-show hostess. ''I like it. Definitely different without being over-the-top.''

''I'm not done with you yet. But since you don't want anything too wild, at least not that's permanent, I'll work a little magic that will disappear with a shampoo.''

Cass produced a large wand with blue bristles and applied it to her hair. Lynn watched as her silver hair took on gleaming blue highlights that framed her face.

''Now to the makeup. I can cover that bruise easily,'' she said, referring to the faint shadow on Lynn's cheek, the reminder of her abductor's cruelty. ''Deep plum lipstick and blush and a vivid blue eyeshadow will be dynamite on you.''

Colors she would never wear in her real life, Lynn thought. When Cass finished the makeup job, and a manicure and pedicure with plum polish, she held out a pair of glasses whose small lenses sans frames were tinted a very pale blue.

"Try these."

"But I don't wear glasses."

"These aren't prescription. Think of them as face jewelry. They'll make your gray eyes appear to be blue."

Indeed, they did. "You're a wonder, Cass."

Lynn had to admit that a colleague very well might pass her in the street without ever giving her a second look. Well, without recognizing her, anyway.

She wondered if Blade would like it.

And then wondered why she wondered. Blade was merely her bodyguard, nothing more. He'd made it quite clear that he wanted nothing more.

So why did she?

Cass altered the direction of Lynn's thoughts by saying, "Now I get to play Barbie and change your wardrobe."

Lynn anxiously wondered what that meant, exactly. While Cass wasn't a small woman, she was model-tall if not quite model-thin. Which meant she couldn't lend Lynn anything. Which meant a shopping spree. Before they left, however, Cass loaned her a couple of bangly bracelets that wrapped around her wrists to hide that reminder of her abduction.

Then Lynn found herself in a series of boutiques she would never have thought of entering on her own. But she also found herself having fun with the free-spirited Cass. And a couple of hours and a long lunch later, she was well contented with a full stomach and several outfits a universe away from her own staid, professional wardrobe.

As she walked down the street in a blue-and-silver-printed sari skirt that hung low on her hips and swirled around her calves, while a silver-threaded white knit top bared her midriff, she felt a little over-exposed.

Even more so when Cass commented, "I think you could carry off a navel ring."

Lynn squirmed. "Getting my ears pierced was traumatic enough."

"Tattoo? It could be temporary."

Lynn glanced in a storefront window and saw nothing of the old Evelyn Cross that anyone would recognize. "I think I'm safe in this disguise."

Truth be told, she hardly recognized herself.

BLADE NEARLY DID a double take when Lynn opened Cass's door to let him in. He whistled appreciatively. "All that was hiding under your lawyer's disguise?"

"The lawyer is the real me," she insisted, though Blade would swear she looked pleased.

"You're sure?"

Flushed with soft color, she murmured, "Thanks."

If he told her any more directly how incredibly sexy she looked, he figured what had almost happened the night before would stand between them. He'd done his best to put her at ease and wanted to keep it that way.

Anything more between them was unthinkable, no matter that his imagination had been sparked by their personal encounter. He had to forget about what had almost happened and remember why he'd volunteered to play bodyguard.

"Maybe I should go into the makeover business," Cass said. "Of course, that would involve licenses.

Which means I would have to go to school so that I could do what I already do really well...oh, never mind.''

''You wouldn't like it, anyway,'' Blade assured her as the women exited the apartment and Cass locked up. ''Instead of being in charge, you'd be at your clients' beck and call.''

''At least *her* clients would be safe,'' Lynn muttered.

''You don't know that,'' Blade said, taking her shopping bags from her and heading down the stairs. ''You don't know what'll set someone off.''

''Sounds like you have experience in that area.''

''More than enough.'' Blade stopped himself before he revealed information about his past in the military that he didn't intend to share. Instead, he murmured, ''People seem to view bartenders as their unofficial therapists.''

''Is that why you're being so generous helping me out?'' Lynn asked.

Her expression was that of a lawyer trying to figure out the angles rather than that of a grateful victim. The last thing he wanted her to do was to probe too deeply as to his motivation. So he chose to practice a little sleight of hand.

''By the way, I tracked down my landlord and made those arrangements for you,'' he said as he opened the outside door and stepped into the courtyard.

''So I'm going to have my own bed tonight.''

Blade noted Lynn's lack of enthusiasm.

''Uh-oh, too much information,'' Cass said, catching up to them.

''She slept on the couch.''

''None of my business.''

But an odd expression crossed Cass's face, as if she knew something she was reluctant to share. Which tied Blade's gut in a knot. His Iroquois grandfather had made him believe that certain people were touched by spirits. People who could see things others couldn't. Though she didn't make a big deal of it, Cass fit that profile. He suspected she knew more about him than he wanted anyone to know.

They arrived at the club early. Team Undercover settled in the break room to powwow, while John Logan photographed Lynn for her new IDs. His attention only half on the conversation, Blade watched his charge smile for the camera.

Evelyn Cross was an eyeful, that was for certain. A woman that beautiful usually knew it, knew how to use it. Amazingly, she seemed oblivious to the fact, perhaps because she'd hidden her real self in her lawyer persona for so long. He wondered why.

Why would a woman that stunning downplay herself...almost as if she were afraid of inviting a man's attention?

She certainly had his, Blade couldn't keep his eyes off her. Or his thoughts.

When Logan finished shooting a roll of film, Lynn joined them at the table.

Gideon said, ''I can have new IDs for you tomorrow, Lynn. Any preference as to name?''

''My mother's maiden name was Parker. Lynn Parker is easy enough to remember.''

''The Parker part's all right, but let's not make the first name so obvious. How about Melinda Parker? We'll introduce you to the rest of the staff as Melinda, and it won't be a big deal if anyone mistakenly calls you Lynn.''

''Fine. But what are the chances that the guy who grabbed me will ever get close enough to get a name?''

''Better to be careful than sorry,'' Blade said.

''I like careful,'' she agreed.

What Blade gathered Lynn didn't like was the idea of working as a waitress.

When Gideon said, ''I'll pair you with one of our experienced wait staff tonight,'' Blade saw a look of displeasure cross her features.

On the one hand, he could understand her reluctance to take on a service job for tips when she made a healthy living as a lawyer. On the other hand…what choice did she really have if she wanted to stay safe?

''Fine,'' Lynn said. ''Cass mentioned something about a uniform.''

''It's not all that bad—a black skirt and a fancy halter top,'' Gideon told her. ''Cass knows where to find them.''

''Great,'' Lynn said without enthusiasm, but she followed Cass out of the lounge without further complaint.

''Is she going to work it?'' Gideon asked.

Blade turned back to his employer. ''She's motivated. And scared.''

''Nothing we can do about the scared part.''

''I'm keeping her close.''

''That you are. The question is…'' Gideon turned his full attention to Blade and asked what he hadn't before when he'd agreed to take Lynn on ''…why?''

''It's personal.''

"I already gathered that. I'm just hoping it's not so personal you make mistakes."

"Too late. I've already made a big one."

One that had altered his life. One that he was desperate to right.

"So this is what?" Gideon asked. "A do-over?"

"You could call it that."

Though the thing he feared most was that no matter what he did, short of giving up his own life, it wouldn't be enough.

AFTER THE PHOTO SHOOT, Gideon had Lynn follow a waiter around for the whole evening. She noted that while she wore a short wrap skirt and a halter top made of a sparkly, jewel-tone-blue material, the dark-haired young man named Todd got away with a more conservative silk T and black trousers. He was a nice kid, though, and he showed her the ropes, including how to use the computer to place food orders, how to work with the mostly foreign kitchen staff to get what she needed and how to deal with the customers.

The music was so loud she could hardly hear him at times. Ironic that the deejay had picked Ashanti's "Happy," because she was anything but.

Her mind kept flitting elsewhere, picking at memories, trying to find something that might help her pin the man who wanted to see her dead. Or at least the one willing to try, she thought as she mentally went over her client list and remembered threats—veiled and otherwise—of ex-husbands and soon-to-be exes unhappy with her.

So as they were locking up the club at one in the morning, she asked Blade, "Can you give me keys to your place? Rather, my new room. I need to go to my office.''

''Now? What's so important?''

''My files. I want to start digging, see if I can make a list of suspects.''

''At this hour?''

''When better?'' Knowing he was going to try to talk her out of it, Lynn dug in her heels. ''During the day, I would have to explain myself to fellow employees. Stella wanted me to think about it. I'm ready now.''

''What about security at the building?'' Blade asked.

''The guards are always changing. They can't keep up with everyone in the place. I have my keys and my identification, so no one should question me.''

Although she was sure her unusual appearance might cause some raised eyebrows.

''You're not going by yourself, Lynn. I'm coming with you.''

Her gratitude that she didn't have to go alone outweighed her irritation that he seemed to be taking charge again, so she didn't argue. ''Thanks.''

Settling into the Jeep, Lynn realized how exhausted she was—and she hadn't even done any actual waitressing. What would the next night be like?

On the drive downtown, she turned her thoughts to the way Blade kept coming to her rescue. Part of her appreciated it, while part of her resented it, because it meant she wasn't really in charge of her own life anymore. The problem being she was stuck with the situation until the villain was brought to justice.

She broke the silence by saying, ''I'm not the type of woman who has to depend on a man.''

"Who said you did? And what would be wrong with that, anyway?"

"A lot. So many women can't fend for themselves that it's unbelievable at times. I actually had a client who not only couldn't tell me what her budget was—I needed to know how high to set the alimony demand—she didn't even know how to balance her own checkbook. No wonder she stayed in a bad marriage until her husband met some little honey and decided he wanted a trade-in."

"And you made him pay."

"You bet I did."

Silent for a moment, Blade said, "You don't seem to like men much."

"I like them well enough. I just don't *trust* them."

"None of us?"

"Well, I trust *you*."

"Why? Because Stella told you to?"

"For one."

"How about for two?"

"You haven't given me reason to *distrust* you."

"I'll bet that wouldn't be too hard," Blade mused.

He had a point. She'd seen too much wrong done to women by men to be unbiased, starting with her own parents. And her work had convinced her that women hadn't really come a long way when it came to personal relationships. Lynn knew she was always wary, always waiting for the proverbial shoe to drop.

"So what happened? Did some guy you were crazy about dump you?"

"I choose to be the dumper rather than the dumpee," she said lightly.

"Often?"

He made it sound as if she'd had scores of men in

her life, when in fact she could count the repeaters on one hand, not one of whom had been charismatic enough to make her lose her head and plunge into a relationship with any fervor.

"Always before things get too serious," she said. "That way, no one gets hurt."

"But if you don't ever take a chance, you can't know where a relationship will go. What if you miss out on something really special?"

"You're a romantic? Blade, I wouldn't have guessed…but, um, I don't see you wearing a wedding ring. And you haven't mentioned anyone special in *your* life."

That stopped him from pressing her.

They rode in silence for a while. Lynn tried to get a sense of Blade's mood, but as usual, he kept to himself. Whatever he was thinking, she couldn't tell. As her office building came into view amid the high-rises west of the Loop, something made her try to explain.

"I do have my reasons for feeling the way I do. My mother couldn't make it without a man. And my father took advantage of that every chance he could."

"He hit her?"

"Not with his fists. With words. He made her feel small and weak and worthless. I never understood why she put up with it. Why she still does. She says she loves him and could never leave him. Now he's living with cancer and he's on another round of chemo. Mom is devoting herself to him and he's treating her worse than ever." She sighed. "If that's love, I don't want anything like it."

"Who says that's what you'll get if you let yourself go?"

"That's what Dani got. My kid sister, Danielle, is a lot like Mom. And unfortunately, she married some- one like Dad. I tried to warn her, but she wouldn't listen to me. She was madly in love. Eventually she got the picture."

"Her husband hit her?"

"No, of course not. Dani never would have stood for that. But her self-esteem certainly suffered. I don't know how long it took me to get her to see the light."

Blade pulled the Jeep next to a parking meter in front of her building. "And then she left him."

"Finally. It's common for women who grow up with any kind of abuse to be attracted to that kind of man."

Lynn's constant fear for herself while growing up.

"But not inevitable," he countered. "It depends on the woman. And you're certainly not weak."

But for some reason, she'd never gotten over her fears in that area.

She gave him a quick look. "You don't even know me."

"I know you well enough."

Did he mean he knew her type? Or would he claim to be psychic like Cass?

"And you still want to help me," she mused.

Cutting the engine, he asked, "Don't you think you're worth it?"

Was she? Sometimes she wasn't certain. Some- times she didn't see clearly enough to make the right decisions. Or to give the right advice. Remembering how wrong she could be sent a chill through her.

"I've made my share of mistakes," she admitted.

"Everyone makes mistakes."

Opening the passenger door, Lynn slid out, saying, "But not ones that get their older sister killed."

Chapter Five

Blade wanted to demand an explanation on that one, but Lynn was too quick for him. She was out of his vehicle and heading for the building's entrance before he could so much as get a word out.

"Better keep up, Blade," she called to him as she went in through the night door. "I work fast. You don't want to get left behind."

Blade hurried and caught up to her as she stopped at the security desk. The guard was young, fresh-cheeked, probably barely legal. And he was staring at Lynn in amazement. Mostly at the flesh bared by the midriff top, Blade realized, noting where his gaze was aimed.

Blade cleared his throat and the kid looked up guiltily, asking, "Can I help you?"

"You're new, Keith," Lynn stated, obviously getting the name from the tag on his shirt. She pulled out her identification. "Or you would know I work late quite often. Evelyn Cross."

The guard started. "It's the middle of the night." His eyes flicked from her to the photo ID. "That don't look like you."

"I've been out on the town. I don't wear my civvies 24/7. Look at the face," she said, brushing the hair back on one side, "not at the stomach."

Lynn was rising above the disguise to her professional self, Blade thought, enjoying watching her work.

The guard flushed and did as she asked. "Yeah, okay, I guess it is you." He seemed agitated as he pushed a clipboard and pen at her. "You need to sign yourself in and out." He looked to Blade. "What about him?"

Lynn scribbled her signature and time and handed Blade the clipboard. "Apparently, he's with me."

She was all business and in charge, quite a turn-around from the frightened woman determined to run.

As they moved away from the desk, Lynn whispered, "Either they're getting younger or I'm getting older."

"Just old enough to handle that well."

Blade couldn't help but be impressed. Then again, he knew Evelyn Cross was good at what she did. He'd made the effort to learn everything he could about her legal practice while she was having her makeover.

Once in the elevator on the way to floor seventeen, Blade wondered what it might be like to work in a high-rise and be required to wear a suit and tie every day. Not anything he could see himself doing. Always a physical, outdoor type, he'd actually liked his long stint in the military...if not always what he'd had to do for the government, particularly not his last assignment.

Which brought him back to the statement Lynn had made as she'd left the Jeep.

"That comment about your sister—"

"I shouldn't have said anything."

"But you did. Obviously it's bothering you, so you need to talk about it," Blade insisted. "What happened?"

She sighed. "Lorraine was a social worker. I had a client living in a culture that pretty much kept her— all their women—from the real world, but somehow she came to me about a divorce. And then she changed her mind. I thought she was either being coerced or she was afraid of what would happen to her and her children if she left her husband, so I asked my sister to talk to her, to give her advice about shelters and programs for displaced women. Because of me, Lorraine ended up being in the wrong place at the wrong time. And now she's dead."

The elevator doors opened and Blade stood frozen. "But you weren't responsible for—"

"Yes, I was. I sent her into that neighborhood, where she was shot and killed on the street. And the bastard who did it was never brought to justice. He was never even identified. But I'm equally guilty because I'm the one who sent Lorraine to her death."

She would never forgive the man who'd pulled the trigger, Blade thought, his gut tied up tight, not when she couldn't forgive herself.

What would she do when she found out the truth?

That he was the bastard who had mistakenly killed Lorraine Cross.

ONCE IN HER OFFICE—spacious, carpeted and filled with classic wood furniture and plants the receptionist watered—Lynn went directly to the file drawers lining one wall. There, she pulled nearly a dozen folders pertaining to cases she'd either taken on or settled in the last year or so and set them on her cherry-wood desk.

"So where do we start?" Blade asked. He'd entrenched himself in one of the upholstered client chairs across from her.

"You don't. These are confidential records. At least some information related to my clients may be confidential." Besides which, she wanted to feel as if she was in charge of some part of her life. "Information pinning down the whereabouts of their spouses is another matter. I have no obligation to them, certainly."

Concentrating, she quickly considered each case that she'd retrieved, going over her copious notes. Fortunately, she always kept track not only of her thoughts, but of the threats from disgruntled spouses that seemed to be part of the job. That was the thing—most of them were bigger talkers than doers.

How did she decide whether a man was a true threat or not?

She noticed that Blade was even more into his low-key mode. Perhaps because he was taken aback by her admission of guilt in her sister's death? Nearly two years had gone by and she still didn't have closure. She would probably never know her sister's murderer. Would probably always carry the blame squarely on her own shoulders.

Lynn couldn't help but wonder if the Cross sisters had each been born with big *V*s for *victim* inscribed across their foreheads. Lorraine hadn't played the victim any more than Lynn herself had, and what made her sister's death even more tragic was that she'd been killed while going to someone else's aid.

Forcing away the dark thoughts, Lynn concentrated on the files before her.

Rather, she concentrated as best she could, considering Blade was watching her every move. She felt his dark gaze wash over her, as intimate as any caress. Heat flushed up her neck and into her cheeks, and she only hoped that he didn't notice. Then again, he claimed to be aware of everything around him, so she was probably doomed.

Not that he said a thing.

Even so, she found herself twitching with awareness of him as she did a cursory sweep of each folder and divided them into two piles, easily dismissing several candidates as she visualized them. One was too short to have been the man who'd grabbed her. Another too heavy. A third too slight in build. That left eight possibles.

Through lowered lashes, she glanced at Blade, who seemed to be studying the details of her office as she studied him. He was a stunning-looking man, cover-model handsome with a body like Adonis. A sudden memory of her hands on his naked flesh made her squirm in her chair.

"Problem?" he asked, his attention focused on her once more.

"Of course I have a problem. I have to figure out which of these men could want to do more than fantasize revenge against me."

"This is a job for Stella and her partner. She's probably been through those files already."

Even though she knew Stella had planned on talking to everyone in the office, Lynn laughed. "You don't know the partners in this firm." They could be very protective of their clients. They wouldn't give away the store, that was for certain.

"They wouldn't cooperate with the police?"

"Only so far as they need to. Besides, no one really knows the details of encounters with a client's angry spouse like the lawyer who handled that particular case. If anyone is going to give your detective friend something solid to go on, it'll be me."

Not that she planned to hand over her list, then sit back and wait. This was *her* life and she would do what she must to protect herself.

"Besides which," she mumbled, "who else would know whether or not these guys wore glasses." Her only lead so far.

Forcing herself to ignore Blade, Lynn went back over the pile, eliminating two more possibilities, men whom she believed didn't have the backbone to stand up to a strong woman, no matter their threats.

"That leaves six potential suspects," she muttered, spinning in her chair to access her computer. "I'm going to bring up their records."

She eliminated two more candidates, both behind in child support payments, when she found one was in jail and the other had returned to his native country.

For the remaining four, she printed up all the information she had about them—one copy for her, the other for Detective Jacobek. But in the end, Lynn eliminated one of those, as well.

"Three candidates," she told Blade, pushing the information toward him.

Rather than reading, he said, "Why don't you tell me about them."

"Victor Churchill, owner of V.C. Technology. He

also owns this building, and he's my highest-profile case ever.''

"Something about that name...I know it.''

"Because it was in the news. He'd been siphoning off marital monies without his wife's knowledge. We found them and Carol got substantially more than she might have if he'd dealt honestly with her in the first place. The judge took offense on her behalf. And then there was an official and well-documented investigation into his business practices. Churchill wasn't happy. The woman for whom he left his wife wasn't happy, either. She left him.''

"Which made him even unhappier with you.''

She nodded. "He promised to ruin me. He wasn't specific as to how.''

"Who's next?'' Blade asked.

"Johnny Rincon.''

"I know him from the old neighborhood.''

"Right. Stella said she knew his ex-wife Carla whom I represented, so I guess that means you did, too. It doesn't sound as if you like Johnny much.''

"When we were in high school, he tried forcing Stella and me into a gang.''

"So what did you do?''

"I cut him.''

He spoke of violence so quietly, so matter-of-factly, that it sent a chill up her spine.

"Rincon called me a whore and said that I would be getting what I deserved.''

"You were raped?''

"No. The man who abducted me didn't touch me sexually. Maybe that means Rincon *wasn't* the one. He's worn sunglasses every time I've seen him, but the attack was at night—''

"Don't underestimate Johnny," Blade warned her. "He's unpredictable. He was dangerous even back then...."

But apparently Blade had been equally or more dangerous. And probably still was, she thought.

"Who's suspect number three?"

"Someone your friend Stella's not going to want to know about."

"On the force?"

"Unfortunately. Roger Wheeler has a reputation for treating offenders with less than respect. When he brought that attitude home, his wife turned him in, said he bragged about the way he got off beating offenders. She's afraid for her kids and we're asking for full custody."

"So this case is still pending. Wheeler threatened you how?"

"He told me that if he had his way, I would regret the day I'd been born."

She gathered her folders and sorted them alphabetically for the file drawers.

"What about that one?" Blade indicated the last data sheet she'd eliminated.

"Timothy Cooper? I don't think so."

"Why not?"

"One, he doesn't wear glasses—"

"That you know of," Blade countered.

"All right. I never saw him wear any. And second, he never physically abused his wife or kids—"

"Again, that you know of."

"I don't see how Sharon Cooper could have hidden that from me. Besides, she cited irreconcilable differences."

"But if you pulled his folder, he must have made

some kind of threat, right? Or you wouldn't have included him.''

''I'm sure he's all talk. He's a chef, for heaven's sake.'' Lynn's stomach lurched as she recalled the spooky man. ''Although he did say he'd like to eat my organs with a nice Chianti.''

''A Hannibal Lecter wannabe.'' Blade whipped up Cooper's data sheet and put it with the other three. ''That's it then, right?''

''I can't think of anyone else. Before we leave, though, I need to check my calendar and my phone messages in case something important has come up.''

''Go ahead.''

She'd barely turned a few pages of her desk calendar before it hit her. ''The Wheeler case—I forgot it goes to court on Thursday.'' And she highly doubted her abductor would be behind bars by then.

''Let someone else handle it.''

''I don't work that way.''

''Then reschedule.''

Thinking about Julie Wheeler, how desperate the poor woman was to end the marriage and hopefully feel safe, Lynn shook her head. ''I can't. Wheeler's had it put off several times. It would be irresponsible of me to put it off yet again. I have to do this, Blade.''

Though he glowered at her, he seemed to understand, saying, ''Then I'll be with you in that courtroom.''

''Thanks. Julie Wheeler would thank you, also, I'm sure, if she knew what was going on.''

Lynn wrote a quick note to the administrative assistant to the effect that she would be at court on Thursday, and that she was taking the file with her now. After slipping the note in the woman's in box, she fetched the file and set it with her "research."

"Now, let me get to my voice mail and I'll be ready to go," she said.

While Lynn dialed in, Blade continued to go over the data sheets on the suspects, as if he were memorizing every detail. His seeming dedication to her situation gave her a confidence she didn't think she would have on her own.

"Three messages," she murmured, grabbing up a pen.

The first was from a client who was angry that her husband wasn't readily agreeing to the terms of child support they'd asked for.

The second was from Julie Wheeler, the cop's wife.

"I'm afraid, Miss Cross. He told me what I could do with the court order, said that he would see his kids anytime he wanted. I read in the papers what happened to you. You don't think he…" She started to cry.

"Whoa," Lynn said softly. "Let me put this on speakerphone."

She replayed the message for Blade, whose expression darkened as he listened.

"Sounds like this guy's got some real anger issues," he said. "Stella needs to hear that message. And as to going to court Thursday—"

"I'm going. This convinces me."

Even as she made sure the message was saved, Lynn felt odd sharing so much about a client. "I'm sure it'll be okay with Julie, or she wouldn't have been concerned enough to warn me."

Then she played the third and final message.

"So, have you returned to the scene of the crime, Evelyn?"

She'd forgotten to turn off the speakerphone and the familiar whisper filled the room and raised the hairs at the back of her neck.

"Or are you picking up this message from some safe place?"

"My, God, that's him."

"No place is safe enough to keep you from me," the recorded whisper went on. *"I'll find you, Evelyn, and when I do…"*

Hearing the click indicating the end of the message, she murmured, "Until we meet again."

Hand shaking, she punched in the code to save the message, as well.

"What does that mean?" Blade asked.

"It means that he's still planning to kill me. And I need to find a way to defend myself."

"You have me."

"A fact that I appreciate. But what about when you're not looking?"

"If it would make you feel better, I can teach you some moves so you can protect yourself."

Though she thought a gun might be more effective, she'd always hated them. And, of course, carrying one that hadn't been registered a lifetime ago was illegal in the city of Chicago. But so was abducting someone and terrorizing her with imminent death.

"I'm a fast learner," she promised him. Though she abhorred violence, she had to be able to protect herself.

"Good. Now about the messages…"

"I have a tape recorder," she said, pulling from a drawer a small one she sometimes used for her work.

"I'm going to make copies before something can happen to them."

In the end, she replayed the messages and recorded them twice, once for the authorities, once for herself. She hadn't given up on figuring out for herself which man was guilty.

"That's it." Lynn threw the recorder and the tapes into her bag.

Blade indicated the data sheets on the disgruntled exes. "Did you ever report these threats?"

"Why would I unless I thought the guy was serious?"

"How many have you thought serious enough to report?"

"Only a couple," she admitted. "When nothing ever came of the threats…"

"Maybe you'd better print up information on the rest of these," Blade said. "Just in case you underestimated the wrong guy."

Feeling as if she were spinning out of control once more, Lynn did as he suggested.

How many deadly mistakes could she afford to make?

That thought echoed through her mind as she finished up. She tried to hide her renewed uncertainty, but inside, she had the jitters.

Her case of nerves didn't dissipate during the elevator ride down with Blade. And they intensified when they stepped into the lobby with its windowed walls to the street. Her attacker could be out there, waiting for her, just as he had been on Friday night.

''That didn't take long,'' the guard observed, sounding surprised.

Lynn said, ''I just needed to get some paperwork.''

Signing out first, she heard her abductor's whispered voice.

Until we meet again...

Not here, not now, she thought, getting herself firmly under control. Any danger was in her own mind. Surely he wouldn't return to the scene of the crime.

THE YOUNG, CLUELESS GUARD had alerted him as he'd been instructed to do. She was inside.

Waiting in the shadows, he got a glimpse of a woman moving away from the security desk. He started when he saw that she *wasn't* Evelyn Cross.

Then he looked again.

The trappings were different, but the way she moved... Besides, who else would be inside in the wee hours of the morning?

A disguise... How clever of her.

He had to give her credit. If he'd simply seen her on the street, he would never have recognized her. Too bad her effort to evade him was for nothing.

She reached the door....

He started to make his move—

Then stopped dead in his tracks when he saw the man who was following her. What the hell! She wasn't alone!

Backing into the shadows, he narrowed his gaze and watched as they left the building, the man's protective arm encircling her shoulders all the way to the

Jeep. She appeared nervous, as well she should. But when she looked around as if trying to spot him, he was like the mist, disappearing into the night.

He took it all in, committed every detail to memory, controlled his growing frustration and rage.

So she'd called in the reserves. Too bad it wouldn't save her. She was too arrogant to lie low. She would make a mistake and he would be there.

The Jeep drove off and he whispered, "Until we meet again, Evelyn…"

LYNN WAS HAVING TROUBLE shaking the jitters. Returning to the scene of the crime had really agitated her. She'd felt him, had imagined he'd been watching her every move, all the way to the Jeep. Ridiculous, she knew.

Upon entering the studio next to Blade's, she said, "This place is almost exactly like yours. Minus the plants."

"And minus the linens. But I have extras," he said, opening the door to her bathroom, which also looked familiar.

To her amazement, he walked through the bathroom, opened the door on the other wall and went into his own quarters.

She followed him but stopped in the doorway. "Um, am I crazy, or is this *your* bathroom?"

"It's *our* bathroom. Dorm-style living. Normally the baths are shared by same-sex renters, but the landlord made an exception for you since I said it was all right with both of us. Which I assume it is, right?"

"I guess so," she said, wondering at the unusual living conditions.

"This place was supposed to be temporary for me," Blade said, as if he could read her thoughts. "I just haven't been motivated to move on." He handed her a set of sheets. "The towels are there," he said, pointing to a stack on a bathroom shelf. "Just remember when you're using it to give me a heads up before you close my door so I don't accidentally walk in on you. And then remember to open the door a crack when you're done."

"Right."

The setup was odd—her sharing a bathroom with a man, one to whom she was perversely attracted. In a way, the notion of being that close to Blade every night was intimidating. In another way, she was reassured that if anything happened—if her abductor somehow traced her back to this place—help was just on the other side of a connecting door.

"It's been a long day. Get some sleep."

"I *should* be sleepy," she said with a sigh. Unfortunately, she was wired instead.

"Tea?" Blade suggested.

"Please."

Wondering how she could figure out which of the men was guilty, Lynn followed him back into his living quarters and paced the length of the room, all the while watching him make her what she hoped would be a quick fix. She still had the jitters. Maybe talking would help.

"I've been thinking about our list of suspects and wondering if I might not be able to do more with that information than Stella," Lynn said. "Besides, what if she scares off the bastard who abducted me, and he covers his tracks? Then I would get no sense of closure. No justice."

"That sounds alarming." Blade punched the microwave keypad and turned his full attention to her. "What do you have in mind?"

Under his close scrutiny, she flushed. "Just checking a few things out on my own."

Not that she'd figured out how. Not yet. But she was a smart woman. A lawyer. She had resources. There had to be something she could do to help herself.

"You're not thinking of using yourself as bait?" Blade's expression darkened. "Because if Johnny Rincon was your abductor, you might just disappear again, for good this time. Better off leaving the cop work to Stella." The microwave dinged and he removed her mug and added a heaping spoonful of herbs. "She knows how to handle guys like him and she'll have the proper backup."

"You're right, of course." Though that didn't mean Lynn had to sit back and do nothing. The more people working on this, the quicker the resolution. "I'll call her first thing in the morning."

"Good," he said, handing her the mug. "Now drink up and then get some sleep."

Easier said than done, she thought an hour later when she was still wide awake. Deciding that lying in the little alcove was giving her claustrophobia, she moved from the bed to the couch.

She honed in on her own breathing, tried to use the

steady sound to clear her mind of everything. But every time she was about to drift off, she flashed on the abduction.

You're the one who does all the talking....

She shifted to her other side and attempted to get comfortable.

Think about what you've done, Evelyn....

She hadn't done anything she hadn't been paid for. Or, in the case of women like Carla, been asked to do.

What had been the most valuable to one of those men? she wondered. His money? His children? Or his simply having a woman to abuse? Which had given some twisted mind incentive enough to abduct her, threaten her, stalk her?

If only she could remember something more about the abduction itself. Some detail more significant than a pair of glasses that could point her in the right direction.

What she needed was a good night's sleep. Then maybe she could think more clearly. But apparently, it wasn't to be.

The newest message roiled endlessly in her head.

No place is safe enough to keep you from me....

She drew her knees up to her chest and made herself small, as if that would keep him from finding her.

Until we meet again...

Unable to help herself, she focused on the event, on her abductor's voice. She concentrated, tried to hear what he was saying to her. Tried to pick up some clue.

...after what you made me lose...

...deserve whatever you get...

Fragments of accusations and threats, nothing more. Nothing new. Nothing that told her what he had lost.

Wife, children, money—which was it? Was she dealing with a man of great wealth? A man who was hand in glove with the authorities who were supposed to help her? A man who'd lived his life breaking the law?

Or could it be a crazy chef who wanted to make cannibal appetizers out of her? she wondered grimly.

What the heck was wrong with her? Why couldn't she turn it all off and sleep? That tea had worked wonders the night before, so why not tonight? Or maybe the security of having Blade so close had been the magic ingredient.

She told herself not to be such a dolt, that Blade was practically in the next room, right on the other side of a couple of doors...doors she could easily open.

As she tried to settle down, tried to make her mind a blank so she could sleep, the thought plagued her: safety was just a few steps away.

Rising from the couch, she took those few steps. The rooms were dark, but her eyes had grown accustomed to the shadows, so she didn't hesitate until she stood in the bathroom and realized her heart was pounding, no doubt because she would feel foolish if he knew what she was about.

Deciding she would take that chance, she slipped into Blade's room, stopped and listened for a moment. The soft snore coming from the alcove told her that he was fast asleep. And when she heard him roll over and the snoring faded into a sigh of contentment, she smiled.

Feeling safer already, she curled up on the couch and listened to the melodic sound of his breathing. Within minutes, her eyes grew heavy and she felt herself drifting...

...until insistent light attacked her lids and she opened her eyes to daylight.

Well, dawn, anyway.

Slowly it came to her that she was on a couch. Blade's couch. Time to get back to her own room.

Concentrating, she listened for any sound from her protector. Nothing.

Now what? What if he was lying there awake, knowing she had crept into his room like some coward?

With a sense of dread, she peeked over the top of the couch to the alcove where Blade lay, dead asleep. He was on his stomach and the sheet was twisted so that it barely covered his butt. One cheek peeked back at her.

No underwear.

Flushing, she tore her glance away from the fine sight and attempted her getaway. Though she tried not to make a sound, she heard Blade stir, and just as she reached the bathroom door, she glanced back to see him roll over. The sheet didn't come with him.

Her mouth went dry and she stared for just a moment. How could she not when such potent masculine beauty was bared to her gaze?

Lynn felt her body responding to his...and then

realized she was engaging in a horrible violation of his privacy.

Ashamed of herself, of the arousal she felt for someone who had no interest in her—he'd made that very clear the other night—she whipped into the bathroom and crossed back into her quarters.

The last thing she needed was for Blade to quit on her in disgust. He was her link to the real world. To sanity. To safety.

She didn't know what she would do without him.

Horrified, Lynn realized how quickly she'd come to depend on a man, and only hoped she never had reason for regret.

Chapter Six

Blade and Lynn arrived at his local gym a few hours later. Though the place didn't appear to be upscale, it was freshly painted and the locker rooms were in good order. Over in one corner of the main gym, a couple of guys were sparring. And in another, a young woman was attacking a punching bag.

Taking possession of a matted area in the middle, Blade told her, "The human foot is made up of twenty-six bones tied together by ligaments."

"And I need to know this why?"

Lynn suddenly wondered if this weren't a mistake—her getting this close to Blade, with potential physical contact involved. She wished they'd successfully reached Stella Jacobek. Instead, they'd had to leave a message for the detective, telling her where they would be.

"The toughest bone, the least likely to sustain damage, is your heel," Blade explained. "You can use it as a weapon against the weaker bones of your assailant's foot."

"You mean just try to stomp on him."

"Yep."

Her stomach curled at the thought of inflicting violence on anyone, even someone with bad intentions. "I needed to come to a gym to learn that?"

"You have to know what you're doing first. Practice makes perfect. C'mon over here and turn around."

Wearing a pair of spandex shorts and a sleeveless T-shirt that showed off his perfect musculature, Blade was too dangerously tempting for her peace of mind. But how could she avoid him after she'd agreed that he should teach her to defend herself?

So Lynn did as he asked, and Blade moved right up against her, the feel of him behind her, solid and male, making the breath catch in her throat and her mouth go dry.

"Now pretend I'm an assailant…"

"Uh-huh."

"…and that I've come up behind you to grab you."

"Okay."

"There's a good chance that I'll have your hands, wrists or arms pinned and out of commission."

He demonstrated, surrounding her and effectively trapping her arms to her sides. Great. She felt every inch of him against her, and part of her wanted to melt, to let her knees go weak so that she could lean on him more fully and enjoy the physical contact.

But the other part of her fought to keep her mind on strategy.

"So, as your assailant," he murmured in her ear, "I've effectively removed two of your most powerful weapons—hands and elbows."

Forcing herself to concentrate, she said, "But I still have my legs and feet."

"And you can easily break the small bones of *my* feet, no matter which way you're actually facing."

"Break? You want me to break bones?"

"Not *mine*," he emphasized. "I was using me as an example. I mean an assailant's. If you're in a life or death situation, you won't have time to be squeamish. You can't let yourself think about it."

"Right. So how do I make sure I don't miss?"

"Let's walk through it. Slowly. No actual violence."

Blade was snugged so close to her his breath feathered the back of her ear. Lynn wanted to tell him to stop, to give her some breathing room, for heaven's sake, but she couldn't humiliate herself like that. She didn't want him to know that he was getting to her. Obviously, this was all business to him, nothing personal.

He continued, "Bring your knee up as far as you can and then slam your foot downward. Flex your ankle so your heel hits first, in a mule kick. Whether you contact the shin or the more vulnerable knee, let your heel slide down your assailant's leg and onto the bones of his foot. Remember to put as much force behind that kick and stomp as hard as you can. Not now, though," he cautioned. "I simply want you to go through the motions very slowly."

"I'll try not to hurt you," she said wryly.

Though an actual weapon might be more effective in her case, Lynn thought. At least her waving a gun around might make a potential attacker back off and give her the chance to run and get help.

Stoically, she attempted the motions Blade described, and felt her glutes rub up against his hip. The sensation spread to more tender parts and she bit back a gasp.

"Good," he said approvingly, seemingly unaffected. "Now let's do it again, a little more quickly, starting with my approach, but—"

"I know, hold back."

"I just want you to get the idea today."

"I'm getting some ideas, all right," she mumbled, though they had nothing to do with self-defense.

When Blade approached her from behind and grabbed her, Lynn ignored the renewed sensations that spiraled through her and did everything he'd asked. And even though it was a mock attack, with no force involved, being able to carry through made her feel a bit better.

"Good," Blade said, but he still didn't let go.

Pulse trilling an unfamiliar song, she asked, "So what's next?"

"If you've been lucky enough to do some damage, his grip will loosen and he'll be more vulnerable. You can use your head as a battering ram against your assailant's nose or mouth. Try it, but again, pull your punch."

Angling her head back as he'd asked, making contact with his face, she was reminded of her struggle with her real attacker and the crack of his glasses.

And suddenly, all personal thoughts scattered.

…payback time, Evelyn….

Freezing, she concentrated on the memory fragment in hopes that more would come back to her.

"Are you okay? Did you hurt something?"

"What?" Snapping out of the moment, Lynn realized Blade had let go of her. "I—I'm fine. I just had another flash. He told me it was payback time."

"Anything else?"

Stymied, she shook her head. "It keeps coming back to me in tiny bits, like the pieces of a puzzle. Nothing I can get a handle on."

"You want to sit?"

"I want to work off this frustration!" she said, refusing to cave in to the fear that was so close now she could taste it. "So how many bones in the hand?"

Blade went through the physiology and then explained that her grabbing a single finger—the pinkie or ring finger, if possible—was most effective. With a sharp motion down and back, she could break it. Again he demanded a walk-through demo.

She complied, then said, "This isn't helping."

"You don't want to know different ways of defending yourself?"

"I want action. I want to feel some sense of accomplishment."

"I'll need some substantial padding before we make it more real. I was planning to do that next time."

"So we're done, then?"

"How about I show you one more?" he said. "Say I don't come up and grab you from behind like before, but I grab on to your wrist like this."

He demonstrated.

"I kick you in the knee? Stomp your foot?"

"I had something else in mind," he said. "Pull your arm down and around to break the hold. Then grab my wrist, pull it up and move into me, passing under our arms. When you cross to the other side, jerk my arm down to pull me over."

"Sounds interesting." But equally unsatisfying if she couldn't carry through.

As if he could read her thoughts, Blade said, "Don't pretend this time. See if you can throw me."

A tempting offer. But considering his size, she doubted she could manage it. "Right."

"C'mon, Lynn, show me what you're made of," Blade challenged. "Start walking and I'll intercept you."

Sighing, Lynn did as Blade asked, and when he came up alongside her and grabbed her wrist, she broke the hold, grabbed his wrist and moved into him just the way he'd shown her. She went under their raised arms, jerked his arm down, and the next thing she knew, Blade was flipping toward the ground. He slapped his hand on the mat to cushion his fall, somewhat the same way he had in her apartment when she'd accidentally pulled him over.

She couldn't help herself....

Taking advantage of his position, she threw her weight against his hip and knocked him onto his back. Continuing the attack, she landed with knees straddling his waist. Adrenaline shot through her.

And a sense of euphoria that made her laugh. Below her, Blade laughed, too.

And then their gazes caught and held. The bubbling laughter churned into something deeper, darker, more primal. And if Blade's gaze were any indication, he was feeling the same. Chemistry...she'd never felt it so strongly with any other man, and she was surprised to discover the feeling might be mutual.

Suddenly self-conscious, Lynn was about to get off Blade when she sensed a presence behind her.

"Are you two gonna be messing around every time I find you together?"

It seemed that Detective Jacobek had gotten Blade's message about where to find them.

BLADE STOICALLY SUFFERED Stella's continuing amusement at a local deli, where they shared a meal, Lynn's suspect list and the new tape recordings. Every time his old friend glanced his way, though, a knowing grin that had nothing to do with this case and everything to do with his personal life curved her lips.

Stella took the heat off him for a moment when she turned to Lynn. "I'm surprised that you took a chance going back to the scene of...uh, your office building."

"I had protection."

Stella grinned at Blade again. "It seems you two have bonded, and in barely more than a day."

Blade noted that Lynn could hardly look at him.

Hell, he was having trouble looking at her, if for a very different reason. Something had clicked between them on that mat—not for the first time—but he wasn't supposed to get involved with her. He *couldn't* get involved with her. That would mean he would have to share his past, and he wasn't ready to do that, especially not with her.

So of all the women he'd seen in the past year— and there had been enough—why did Evelyn Cross suddenly have to be the only one he wanted?

"Lynn and I want the same thing," he told Stella.

"Do you?"

He gave her a dark look and growled, "Justice and Lynn's safety."

"Uh, right." Stella gave Lynn a thorough once-over. "I guess this, um, disguise is part of the deal."

"Who would recognize her?" Blade said agreeably.

"What did you do?" Stella asked Lynn directly, "study fashion magazines?"

When Blade answered, "Something like that," before Lynn could bring up Cass, Stella gave him an odd look.

Having finished her sandwich, she returned to scrutinizing the data sheets. "One of your colleagues mentioned Victor Churchill as a man who always found a way to reduce his enemies. Of course, he meant doing business. Another said Johnny Rincon scared her to death."

"You mean Susan Matthews," Lynn said. "She was talking to me outside the courtroom the day his and Carla's divorce was finalized. He called Susan a not-so-nice name and told her to get lost."

Stella looked at Blade. "Did you tell Lynn about Johnny?"

"I gave her a thumbnail."

"He's scum," the detective warned Lynn. "Dangerous. I wouldn't put it past him to do this to you."

Neither would Blade. That was why he planned on paying the old neighborhood a visit that afternoon. He wanted to learn for himself what Johnny Rincon was up to.

"Did you listen to the tape I gave you the other night?" Lynn asked Stella. "Could that be *his* voice?"

"I did listen. I'm sorry, Lynn, but I can't say that I recognized the voice. Keep in mind it wasn't much to go on and the offender was whispering. Plus it's been years since I've run into Johnny. I did turn it over to the lab, though, to see if there are any distinguishing background noises that could clue us in to his location.''

''I don't see what good that would do unless he was stupid enough to call from home or an office.''

''You're probably right. But just in case, I want to put a tap on your phones to intercept any future calls.''

''Fine with me.''

Stella met Blade's gaze. ''What about you? You heard this one.'' She indicated the tape from the office that Lynn had just given her. ''Familiar?''

''Like you said, he was whispering. And it's been years.''

''Maybe an expert could tell. Maybe. Of course, he'd have to have recordings of them all. Which is a problem unto itself.''

''Why?'' Lynn asked. ''If we had recordings of the suspects and an expert could match up the voices—''

Stella interrupted. ''Unless the guy knows he's being recorded, we're violating his civil rights and the tape wouldn't be admissible in court. Not likely any of these guys will sign off on that one.''

Lynn didn't object, but Blade could see she wanted to. In the end, she let it pass.

''I have something else you should know, Lynn,'' Stella said. ''Some hours after you left your building with Blade, someone broke in.''

''Into my apartment?''

''That's the thing. It seems not. The security guard was knocked out and when he came to, he was trussed up on the office floor. The guys who investigated couldn't come up with anything. The guard had his keys on him. No apartment seemed to be broken into.

No one reported anything. We can't figure out what the guy's purpose was.''

"Then why tell me?"

"Because I don't believe in coincidences. And because one tenant's boyfriend left the building about the same time—the security guard wasn't there, but he thought Tony had taken a break or something. Anyway, he passed another guy going into the elevator and said something didn't seem right to him.''

"What about a description? Is Tony all right?''

"Tony's fine. And that's all we have. No description other than the guy was about six feet tall, with a medium build. He was wearing a billed cap and kept his head down. This morning, I went over there and got the manager to open your apartment for a look-see. Everything appeared exactly as it did when I was there the other night. If anyone paid you a visit…'' She shrugged.

Blade sensed Stella's unease about the situation spread to Lynn. She seemed a little off-kilter after that.

They wound up the lunch meeting promising to take a closer look at their list of suspects. All of them. Lynn didn't know Stella the way he did. His old friend hadn't even blinked at the fact that a cop was on that list. Blade figured she would be harder on a cop than on a civilian if she had reason to believe he was the offender.

But Blade's mind was back on Johnny Rincon when he brought Lynn home.

"You didn't let me do all that much physical stuff,'' she said, "but I'm exhausted anyway.''

"Good, have a lie down or you'll never get through work. You should sleep easier tonight.''

He thought about inviting her to sleep in his room again, but he didn't think she'd appreciate his observation that she had done so the night before. He still slept as he'd been trained to do when in the Special Forces—with part of his brain on the alert for danger. He hadn't let on that he knew, because she'd been very furtive, very protective of her dignity, and he was aware of how important that was to her.

Lynn said, "I need a shower. Should we flip to see who goes first?"

"Be my guest. I need to take care of something."

"You're leaving me here alone?"

"Think of this as a safe house. No one would know to look for you here. You do feel safe here, don't you?"

"With you, yes. When I'm with you, I don't feel like anything could go wrong."

He wanted her to feel safe with him, of course. It was the second part that bothered him. He was far from infallible. He was proof of how wrong things could go. If she ever found out what had happened to her sister…

Before that tragedy, he'd trusted his instincts implicitly. But that one time when it had counted most, his instincts had betrayed him and he'd made a tragic mistake that he never could correct. He would never be able to forget that. He would never be able to trust himself fully again.

"You won't be gone long, will you?" Lynn asked.

"A couple of hours."

He needed time away from her, time to sort things through, to regain perspective. He needed breathing room so that he didn't compound his mistake.

Making sure both outside doors were locked, he

headed down the stairs and got in his Jeep. No one would find Lynn here, he assured himself, wanting to be certain of it.

So Blade headed out for the South Side, remembering the last time he'd seen Johnny Rincon, who still wore the scar he'd given him in high school. The sick bastard had said he liked the way his face looked because it made people fear him.

The old neighborhood hadn't changed much. People littered the stoops and sidewalks in the summer. No matter the box fans and air-conditioners that poked out of apartment windows; the streets were the center of their social lives. Kids played fast and loose with traffic, gangs gathered on corners to discuss "business" and old folks sat on their porches and watched life pass them by.

The main drag was littered with dollar stores, pawn shops and secondhand merchandise, both clothing and furniture. No bookstores or coffee houses or sushi bars here. The neighborhood was a throwback to another time.

One Blade had done his best to leave behind.

He hadn't been back since his mother had moved to the suburbs to live with her sister a half-dozen years before, when his younger sister, Rena, had married. He'd been in the military then. And when he'd left Special Forces more than a year ago, he'd had no desire to return to this place.

He was doing it for Lynn.

Luckily, he found a parking spot near Skipper's. The tavern set back on a side street corner used to be the hotbed where everyone with a reputation or without a steady job gathered. He hoped that was still the case.

Entering, he stopped near the door and looked around the smoke-thick room with its pseudo-maritime interior. Despite the early hour, the tavern was busy, and the owner, Skipper—graying, with a handlebar mustache and thick sideburns poking out from under his ship captain's cap—still held court at the bar with its big wheel at one end. Around a corner table, several guys played cards. And the click of pool balls echoed from the alcove in back. Blade headed in that direction and looked over the participants. Illegal or not, they were playing for money, of course. He wouldn't have expected less.

"Well, look what the wind blew in—Blade Stone," Skipper announced from behind the bar.

The tavern grew hushed and Blade felt the atmosphere charge as all heads turned toward him. He claimed a stool. More than a few of the customers were friends of Johnny's. Or at least they were his associates. In a neighborhood like this, grudges were not soon forgotten. They continued on with a life of their own.

A cell phone flipped open and the owner turned his back on the table as he made his call, while a thin man sporting a goatee threw down his cards.

"I fold," he announced loudly. "You guys are too good for me today."

Rising, he sauntered over to the bar and took a stool next to Blade, who couldn't believe his good luck.

"Big surprise, you showing out of nowhere, Blade. Never thought I'd see your ugly face again."

"If I knew you were going to be here, Leroy, I would have stayed away longer." After returning the insult, Blade grasped the smaller man's hand. "How are you?"

"Thirsty."

"We can fix that." Blade signaled Skipper to get them two beers. "So, same old, same old?"

"Pretty much. Got me two more kids."

"That makes five? Haven't you ever heard of abstinence?"

Leroy laughed and grabbed his beer. "The wife wants to try again for a girl." He chugged down some of the brew, then asked, "How many you got?"

"Never married."

"What's that got to do with anything?"

They laughed, clinked mugs and drank, while Blade shook away the mental image of a tiny blonde with big gray eyes that suddenly came to him.

He spent a few minutes catching up before he ordered two more beers, then moved the conversation to a private table in the corner and took it in the direction he wanted.

"So, is Johnny Rincon still the big man in the neighborhood?" Blade asked in a low voice.

"For some people."

Leroy was Carla's cousin, and with his love of family, he'd never been overly fond of Johnny, the wife-beater.

"I hear Carla dumped him."

"Yeah, she finally got some sense."

"And I hear he wasn't too happy with her attorney."

Leroy swirled the beer in his mug and scrutinized him. "What's this about, Blade?"

"Fishing expedition. Last Friday, someone grabbed

that lawyer and threatened to kill her. She doesn't know who.''

''You think it could be Johnny?''

Blade shrugged.

''What's your interest?'' Leroy asked.

''The lawyer.''

''She hired you?''

''Not exactly. It's personal.''

''Ahh. Ain't seen you this intense since Mary Elizabeth Ferguson.''

A short-lived romance that had ended when he'd joined the military.

About to tell Leroy that it wasn't that kind of personal, Blade stopped himself. The hell it wasn't, he couldn't deny he wanted to be more than Lynn's bodyguard. Besides, it wouldn't hurt to let Leroy think whatever would get him the best answers.

''I don't want anything bad to happen to her,'' Blade said. ''You know how it is when you want to protect a woman.'' As far as Blade knew, Leroy had been true to his Theresa since high school. ''So, was Johnny around last weekend?''

Leroy grew thoughtful. ''Don't know as I saw him. 'Course, I weren't around on Sunday. That's family day. Tell you what I'll do, being that I hate that bastard for what he did to my little cousin and all. I'll ask around, see what I can find out.''

''Find out what?''

The tavern quieted again, as if every man there was holding his breath. Blade felt Johnny's presence behind him like something crawling up his spine. Leroy's expression closed. He might hate his cousin's ex, but he wasn't about to challenge him outright.

"I was telling Blade here I'd ask around, see who has an old Corvette for sale," Leroy said.

It was a bold-faced lie, yet one that was plausible, since Carla's cousin was a mechanic, Blade decided.

"Thought I'd go for something a little easier on the eye than that old Jeep of mine." Blade glanced up at Johnny, then turned back to Leroy, who was getting up from the table. "I particularly like red."

"Like I said, I'll see what I can do for you."

"I'll be in touch."

Leroy waved and sauntered toward the door as if he was in no hurry.

"So, you want a red Corvette."

Johnny moved more directly into Blade's line of sight. He was wearing sunglasses, and didn't remove them despite the low light. He'd been almost handsome once, but the scar that split his right cheek made him look feral, especially when he smiled, as he was doing now.

He flipped a chair around backward and straddled it. The vest he wore over a white T-shirt was loose and probably hiding a holstered gun at his back. Then he snapped his fingers at Skipper without so much as looking the bartender's way.

"I can probably find you whatever you want. How much you willin' to pay?"

Blade just bet Johnny dealt in stolen vehicles and could have anything picked up off the street on command. "I don't think I can afford you."

"Not even if I make you a deal you can't refuse?"

"That's what I'm afraid of. And when the police catch up to me, they'll make me another deal I won't be able to refuse, one entailing jail time."

Johnny threw his head back and laughed. And then

he sobered. The low light over the table threw long shadows over his face, making him appear even more menacing than usual. Skipper set two beers down on the table and Johnny waved him away.

"On me."

"Thanks, Johnny, but two's my limit," Blade told him. "I'm driving."

"Soon, I hope. And when you go, stay away. You got no business in this neighborhood anymore."

"Last I heard, it was still a free country."

"Yeah, I heard you went off to protect it from guys tougher than me. How did that go for you?"

Refusing to be baited, Blade sat back and stared at the other man. Not that he could get through the dark glasses that Johnny wore pretty much 24/7. Lynn hadn't seen her attacker, so she didn't know what kind of glasses he'd been wearing. Just the thought of Johnny's hands on her made Blade's blood boil. If Johnny was guilty, he would have to hold himself back from doing his nemesis personal damage.

"Those new sunglasses?" Blade asked him.

"Thinking of getting some fashion sense?"

"I'm comfortable in my own skin."

"You'd be more comfortable wearing it elsewhere."

"That's the second time you said that, Johnny." Blade spoke in a low growl so that no one else could hear. "Is that a threat?"

Knowing that Johnny was armed and dangerous, Blade let his hand fall toward his leg and the knife strapped there as he stared steadily at his old nemesis.

Suddenly, Johnny laughed again, though he didn't seem in the least amused. "I was just making an observation—you're not one of us anymore."

"I was *never* one of you."

"So what are you doing here in the burg? What is it you're looking for, Blade?"

Sticking to Leroy's story, he said, "A red Corvette, but not from you."

Then he rose and strode over to the bar, where he settled his tab with Skipper. As he left, he felt Johnny Rincon's gaze burning the middle of his back until the door closed behind him.

Blade could only hope the bastard didn't go after Leroy to get the real answer to his question.

Chapter Seven

Showering and washing her hair had put Lynn in a better mood, and so she'd decided to check on her parents, this time in person. If Blade could go off on his own, then she could, too. Only she wanted to do this fast and get back before he did.

Not that she was afraid of his disapproval.

Deciding that freaking out her folks with her disguise would not be a good move, she left applying fresh blue streaks until later and stuffed up the ultra-blond hair under a straw hat that went nicely with a pair of tan slacks and a white top, all from her own wardrobe. A touch-up over the faint bruise left on her cheek and a slash of peach gloss across her lips and she was ready.

At the last minute, she left Blade a note to let him know where she'd gone, just in case he returned before she did.

A taxi left her off on the northwest side of the city, her old monied neighborhood with its wide lots and long lawns and large houses. Unsure of what prompted her desire to enter the two-story Georgian she mostly avoided these days, Lynn felt as if it was fate when she noted the familiar car in the drive, a black Beamer belonging to her ex-brother-in-law.

"What is he doing here?" she muttered. As if she didn't know.

The moment she let herself in through the side door, she heard Nathan Sennet trying to charm her mother.

"C'mon, Mother Cross, give a guy a break. I've changed. I swear I have. Shouldn't Danielle have the chance to see that for herself?"

"Well, I, uh, don't know."

And able to tell her mom was ready to give away the store, Lynn stepped into the kitchen, saying, "I do know. Dani wants nothing to do with you, Nathan. She left the country to get away from you."

Handsome, blond, tanned, charming and successful in business—always an athlete himself, he was a sports agent by profession—Nathan Sennet was many a girl's fantasy. He'd certainly been Dani's.

"Left the country?" His smile faded to a little-boy-lost look. "You mean on vacation? Where to? For how long?"

"Where or why or how long doesn't concern you anymore."

"Of course it concerns me. I love Danielle, for God's sake. I always will. Look, Evelyn, I know you think I'm like your father, but I'm not," he said in a low tone, as if trying to spare her mother's feelings. "I admit we had some problems and maybe I was a little overprotective, but I've been working on my shortcomings with a professional." Seeming anxious that she believe him, he said, "I swear to you that I'm a different person now."

"Good for you."

"Not for me. I've been seeing a psychotherapist for your sister."

"You could have done that last year, when she was still interested in saving your marriage."

"I needed a wake-up call," he admitted. "And I'm doing what I have to now."

"Now is too late."

"That's not for you to say. You have these pre-conceived notions…you can't see what's in front of your nose. But Danielle will want to know that I'm doing this for her. She still loves me."

Lynn knew that to be true. Thankfully, she'd been able to convince Dani to take the job in London, putting enough distance between them so she wouldn't be seduced back to Nathan, compounding her mistake.

"I don't know what I can do to convince you," Nathan said. "I love Danielle with all my heart. She's my life, my world. That's why I've spent the last several months making myself worthy of her love. I'll give you the name of my psychotherapist. Check out my progress for yourself. I'll give him permission to talk to you. Unless you don't want your own sister to be happy."

"Of course I want her to be happy." Torn because he seemed sincere, Lynn said, "Let me think about it and I'll get back to you." She supposed she would have to call Dani and let her decide.

Nathan beamed at her. "That's all I ask." Then his expression grew serious. "Hey, I'm sorry. I'm not even thinking about you. I was shocked when I saw you on the news the other day. I couldn't believe some crazy man abducted you. Thank God you came out of it all right. Have they caught the creep and locked him up?''

"Not yet," she said, her stomach tightening at the reminder.

"Well, until they do, lie low." He patted her arm awkwardly, as if what he really wanted to do was hug her but didn't dare. "Stay safe, okay?"

The moment Nathan was out the door, her mother hugged her and said, "I'm so glad you came, Lynn. I didn't know what to tell him."

"As far as Nathan is concerned, Mom, you can't tell him anything, not unless Dani says she wants him to know where she is." Lynn stepped out of her mother's embrace to look her in the eye.

"He *is* her husband."

"No, Mom, he's not. They're divorced."

"I don't believe in divorce."

Her eternal excuse for sticking by her own husband, Lynn thought. Not that she didn't love her father. He had been a good provider and he could be affectionate and fun when he wasn't in one of his dark moods. Only those moods had shattered their home life too often.

"You look all right," her mother said, her anxious gaze suddenly giving Lynn the once-over. "You are all right?"

"I'm fine. How is Dad today?" Lynn asked, knowing he'd just had another round of chemotherapy, and wanting to be prepared before she went in to see him.

"Poor man, I can't seem to do anything right for him today."

"That's it, Mom, blame yourself, as usual," Lynn muttered.

She crossed through the dining room and into the

living room, where her father was ensconced in a re-clining chair before the television. Dozing, he looked much more vulnerable and thinner than the last time she'd seen him.

"Hey, Dad, how are you doing?" When she leaned over to kiss his cheek, the brim of her hat scraped him.

"Get that thing out of my face," he grumbled. "Why are you wearing that silly hat in the house?"

"I just washed my hair and couldn't do anything with it. You sound like your normal self," she observed. "So you can't be doing too badly."

"I don't need your sarcasm. That mouth of yours is what got you in all that trouble."

"Excuse me?"

"A man doesn't just go off and take a woman hostage for no reason."

Lynn couldn't believe she'd heard him right. "You aren't saying that I deserved to be abducted and have my life threatened, are you?"

"No, honey," her mother assured her, "he's not saying that."

"Don't speak for me, woman."

For once her mother ignored him. "He was so worried over what happened to you he was all agitated. It's just the chemo talking."

Her father wasn't saying anything now. He was staring at his television as if she weren't there.

"No, Mom, it's not the chemo. That's pure Dad. I knew I shouldn't have come here. But it's not too late to correct that mistake." She kissed her mother on the cheek and headed for the door, wanting to get away from this house before she burst into tears.

"Take care of yourself. I'll call you to see how things are going."

She left accompanied only by the sounds of the television.

Once outside, Lynn realized she hadn't called a taxi. So she pulled out her cell phone and did so, then sat on the curb to wait.

How could her father have said such a horrible thing to her? Even Nathan had been more compassionate. Psychotherapy must be doing him good, she admitted grudgingly. Yes, she believed her father had been worried, but this was a pattern she recognized. He got worried or upset about something and he struck out, making it her mother's fault, usually. This time it was Lynn's. Well, her mother might have chosen to put up with it, but she didn't have to follow suit.

Even so, she couldn't help the tears that rolled down her cheeks. She dashed them away with the back of her hand as the Yellow Cab came barreling down the street. And as she settled in the back seat and gave the driver the address, she thought she would give anything to have Blade wrap his arms around her and just hold her.

Lynn barely knew the man, but she felt infinitely more comfortable with him than with any other man in the past who'd come and gone from her life. Wondering why that was, she decided it was probably because he listened, and because he wasn't judgmental. As to control issues, she guessed he had some, but in this case they were understandable since he was trying to keep her safe.

Nathan had told her to stay safe.

How surprising. She and her brother-in-law had

never been fond of each other, though they both had managed to be polite for her sister's sake. Maybe psychotherapy had helped him resolve all kinds of control issues. If, indeed, they had been *his* issues. Lynn wasn't so sure now. Nathan had said she had preconceived notions about him, and he'd denied being like her father. His willingness to work with a psychotherapist proved that, she thought.

Maybe he did deserve another chance. She'd call Dani and talk to her about Nathan.

And she'd have to rethink Blade.

She'd have to rethink her control issues altogether, Lynn decided, suddenly wondering if her father's negative influence had warped her so much that she'd been unfair to any man interested in her. Had she always looked for the negative?

Could she have done that to Nathan, as well?

Startled, Lynn wondered if her own suppositions and her influence on Dani could have done damage to her sister's marriage.

Dear Lord, she hoped not. She'd never wanted to ruin anyone's life.

"Say, *señorita,*" the Hispanic driver called back to her, "you got a friend you want following us?"

"What?" She swiveled in her seat to look out the rear window, and spotted a silver Taurus too far back for her to see anything but a shadow of the driver. "Why do you think he's following us?"

"Been with us since I pick you up. Came off the side street."

"It's probably a coincidence."

But when they made the next turn, the silver Taurus turned as well, and Lynn's pulse picked up.

Could her abductor now be stalking her, waiting
for another chance to finish what he'd started?

Until we meet again...

"He's still with us," the driver announced.

"I know, I know."

As unlikely as it seemed that the villain would be
waiting for her to show up at her parents' home, what
if it were true? Someone had broken into her building,
seemingly for no purpose. What if her abductor had
been the one, and he'd somehow gotten into her
place? Her address book sat on her desk next to her
computer, big as life for anyone to find...

Lynn's heart thundered so hard the rush of her own
pulse filled her ears. Her chest tightened and she felt
as if she couldn't breathe properly.

Thoroughly spooked, she choked out, "Turn right
here and let's see if the other car follows suit."

"Sí, señorita."

She turned in her seat to watch the end of the block
as they zoomed down the street. A moment later, the
silver car made the turn, as well.

"We *are* being followed." Knowing it was her
fault, she tried to stay calm. She'd shown up at her
parents' place minus her new identity—and she'd
played right into his hands. "Can you lose him?"

The driver flashed her a smile. "For you, *señorita,
sí!*"

The taxi shot forward and Lynn grabbed on to the
front seat to steady herself as they whipped around a
corner, narrowly missing an oncoming car. The other
driver slammed on his brakes and blared his horn at
them, started up and came to another dead stop to
avoid the silver car.

The taxi barely paused at the stop sign before barrelling around the corner onto Western Avenue.

"Take a detour!" Lynn yelled above the renewed rush in her ears. "Don't bring him anywhere near Bucktown."

The driver's response was to throw his left arm out the open window, zoom ahead of the SUV next to them and start making a left turn.

"Whoa!" Lynn gasped out. "You can't do that! You're in the right lane!"

But it seemed he could.

Cars moving in both directions came to a screeching halt as he executed the illegal left turn. Seeing that the silver car was stuck in traffic behind the SUV, Lynn prayed that she wouldn't elude her abductor only to be killed in a multivehicle accident.

Miraculously, the taxi flew down the thoroughfare, heading east without incident. A block later, the driver turned back north on a one-way side street, and with a squeal of wheels, took a right and then a left into the heart of a T-shaped alleyway. Halfway down the block, he pulled onto a parking pad behind a small, three-story apartment building.

Unless the other driver followed the taxi's exact route, he would never find them, Lynn realized with relief. Taking her first deep breath since the chase had started, she sagged back into her seat.

"Where did you learn to *do* that?"

The man turned and proudly grinned at her. "For ten years I drive taxi in Mexico City."

GOING CRAZY WITH WAITING, Blade turned himself inside out for leaving Lynn alone. He should have called Cass and asked her to baby-sit their client.

If anything happened to her...

If anything happened to her, he would take it personally, doubly so. Not only did he owe Lynn because of her sister, but truth be told—inappropriate as it might be—he was starting to have feelings beyond the obvious physical attraction for the woman herself.

How could he not when she obviously cared so deeply for other people? When she worked so hard for her clients—not the ones whose pockets were lined with money, but the ones who had nothing to offer but their thanks?

Lynn was as good a person as the sister whose life he'd extinguished.

A hard, cold knot settled in the pit of Blade's stomach as he realized there was nothing he could do but wait. He didn't even know when she'd left. He'd made another stop after leaving the tavern, so he'd been gone longer than he'd meant to be. Not that it was an excuse for her going off on her own. Lynn was an adult who made her own decisions—unadvised as this particular decision might be.

By the time he heard a vehicle pull up in the alley, he was nearly out of his mind with worry. He glanced out the window and saw her alight from a taxi. His heart lifted, but his agitation didn't. He threw himself into a chair and gripped its arms and tuned his mind to an inner voice that kept his emotions from erupting. Listening intently, he caught her footfalls on the outside stairs.

One minute he decided he would make no move to meet her at the door. The next, he was through the bathroom and inside her quarters.

As Lynn's key scraped the lock, he leaned against the back of the couch and crossed his arms over his chest, forcing himself to a calm he really wasn't feeling.

The moment the door opened, Lynn froze and let out a yelp. Then she blinked, and as if just then recognizing him, stepped inside.

"Blade, what are you doing in here?"

"The bigger question is what were you doing out there?"

Visibly perturbed, she flushed with color. "I left you the note—"

"I thought you were going to take a nap."

"That was your idea."

"And a damn good one."

As she slammed the door behind her and moved closer, Lynn's voice rose to an unflattering pitch. "Stop telling me what to do. You're not my boss!"

Disliking her tone, he quietly said, "No, I'm merely your bodyguard."

She threw her hat down on the couch and practically got in his face when she said, "Well, then, act like one!"

Though offended, Blade realized Lynn was deeply upset about something and so he held himself in check. "I thought that was what I was doing—trying to keep you safe. How can I when you won't even stay where I leave you? A criminal doesn't give potential victims a time-out."

At which point Lynn burst into tears, leaving Blade speechless.

What the hell had happened to her?

Blade watched warily as Lynn tried to get herself under control, a seeming impossibility. So he reached out, hooked her shoulder and pulled her toward him.

Still sobbing, Lynn landed against his chest. Then

her arms snaked around his waist and her head landed in the crook of his neck.

What the hell! One minute she was yelling at him, the next she was using him as a human hanky. As he had the other night, he swept his arms around her back and held her close, soothing her with long strokes down her spine until the wracking sobs became tremors. His chest tightened with some unnamed emotion as he held her.

"H-he was there, at my parents' place, waiting for me," she said with a gasp. "He must have knocked out the guard at my high-rise so he could get into my apartment and get at my address book—"

"We need to tell Stella."

Still plastered against him, Lynn nodded. "I didn't mean to cause trouble. I just wanted to check on my folks. That's why I'm wearing my own clothing—so as not to shock them. When I left to come back here, the taxi driver saw the car pull out after us. We evaded him so he doesn't know about this place. He was driving a silver Taurus, Illinois plate number PKM 363 F."

"If that was even his car," Blade murmured, thinking about how easily Johnny Rincon could have lifted one. And wondering if Johnny had had enough time to drive across town and lie in wait for Lynn.

She shuddered against him one last time and lifted her head. Staring down into her gray eyes, cloudy with fear, lashes spiked with tears, he wanted in the worst way to make her forget the terrible thing that had happened to her. He wanted to make her feel safe.

Happy.

His.

And for a moment, when he was unable to stop

himself from brushing his mouth over hers, Lynn *was* his.

She raised up on tiptoe, and even through their garments her tight nipples created intense sensations along his chest. Then she slid her arms around his neck, where her fingernails left a trail of gooseflesh.

Groaning, Blade took possession of her mouth as he wanted to take possession of the rest of her. His body became inflamed as her lush softness pressed against him. Desire nearly overpowered him, but he fought it so that he wouldn't do what he shouldn't. Still, he couldn't resist drawing out the kiss, couldn't stop his hands from touching her possessively.

She was melting into him, sighing against his mouth, her worries apparently forgotten.

Well, he couldn't forget.

Gently, Blade once more pushed Lynn away from him, though he didn't release her. Disappointment flickered across her features, only to disappear in a neutral expression that hid whatever she was thinking. Her lawyer's face? But as usual, he noted, her eyes gave her away. She was confused. Hurt.

"You know I want to keep you safe, right?" he asked softly.

"Yes, of course. As a favor to Stella."

"Leave Stella out of this. I don't want anything more to happen to you."

"Neither do I."

"Then you won't do anything foolish again, right?" he pressed.

"Depends on whose definition of foolish we're using." Her expression stubborn, Lynn backed off.

So Blade tried using logic with her. "Would you

agree that if we were talking about a legal defense, you would have one over me?''

''What's your point?''

''That I'm a lot more familiar with dangerous situations and how to deal with them than you are.''

She crossed her arms over her chest. ''Your idea of dealing with my situation is to do nothing?''

''Protecting you is nothing?''

''I didn't say that.''

''How about giving up sleep to dig through your office files for a lead on your abductor?'' he asked. ''That was barely twelve hours ago. Was that nothing?''

''Well, no, but—''

''And my going back to the old neighborhood to find out if anyone saw Johnny Rincon around this weekend—is *that* nothing?''

She gaped at him for a moment before demanding, ''Why didn't you tell me where you were going?''

''I figured you would insist on coming along. Which, by the way, I wouldn't have allowed.''

''*You* wouldn't have allowed?''

''For your own good.''

She swallowed hard and opened her mouth, but nothing came out.

Not wanting to argue, Blade said, ''We don't have to leave for work for an hour. We could both use some downtime. Not that I'm telling *you* what to do.''

With that, he left Lynn to her thoughts and went back to his own quarters, wondering if she'd learned anything from her scare that afternoon. She was certainly determined to be her own woman.

Part of her appeal, he supposed. She had guts and

kept him guessing. One minute she wanted to be in charge, the next she wanted to depend on him.

Which made him think about the powerful physical attraction between them. Lord, he was only human. He didn't know how much more he could take, comforting her and not taking it further. Even as he wondered what it would be like to let go and lose himself in her, Blade knew he would be taking advantage if he made love to Lynn.

She still didn't know the whole truth about how her sister had died.

A truth that would make her look at him differently. With distrust, perhaps hatred.

A truth he didn't want her to know.

Not ever.

AFTER DRIVING AROUND the North Side until the damn car ran out of gas, he abandoned it. Wiped it free of his prints, got out at the intersection where it had refused to move on a green light, and walked away.

Just as he'd figured she would go back to her office, he'd been right about the bitch showing up at her parents' place. But now that she was forewarned, she probably wouldn't step foot back in that house again.

So where *would* she go? What the hell was she doing with herself while he was going nuts wondering if things were coming back to her, enough to pin the crime on him?

He'd wanted to terrorize her—his specialty—to show her the error of her ways. He'd wanted to strip her of everything she thought she knew about fairness and replace it with an education in revenge. He'd wanted her to be so certain that he would kill her that she would get down on her knees and beg for mercy.

Maybe then, knowing she was broken as she should be, he would have spared her.

But not now.

Not when she continued to defy him at every turn.

Not when she kept cheating him of his victory.

Someone knew where she was holed up: Stella Jacobek. So what if she was a cop? She was a woman first.

He smiled at the new direction his thoughts took, certain there had to be a way to make her talk.

Chapter Eight

"Three wild Jacks from the suburbs were lost trying to find their way through Chicago, and decided the best way to get help was to go in different directions," the Amazing Cassandra told the volunteer who'd joined her onstage at Club Undercover.

Having recovered from her emotional outburst, Lynn was glad to be keeping busy, even if it was working as a waitress. While delivering a tray of drinks to a table, she kept an ear out for Cass's patter that accompanied her card trick.

"The first one to get help would come rescue the others." Cass waved the three cards from the deck she was holding. "So off they went."

Cass certainly had the audience involved, Lynn thought, as she set down a beer in front of a customer. He was staring at the stage, fixated on the vision in scarlet, and grinning like an idiot. As were most of the male customers, she noted, even those with dates.

"All right, sir, would you place one jack on top of the pack," Cass said, "one in the middle and the last jack on the bottom. Then cut the deck."

Finished distributing the drinks, Lynn glanced up as Cass made a big show of waving a wand over the deck, adding a little hip action that drew laughs from the crowd. Then she turned the pack face up and spread the cards to show three jacks together near the center.

"So the friends got back together and all came to Club Undercover for some hot music and dancing! Maestro!" Cass called to the deejay.

Music blasted through the room and the audience cheered as Cass took a bow, her wide smile lighting her face. She was used to this, Lynn thought. She ate it up. And she had incredible chemistry, not only with men but with the women, as well. Despite her stunning good looks, Cass had a way about her that was nonthreatening.

A realization that made Lynn wonder why she was working in a small club rather than on the professional stage.

The grinding sounds of techno-rock filled the space and Lynn wondered about getting earplugs. That might help her nerves, but how was she supposed to hear the customers' orders? She rushed back to the bar to fill another.

As Blade set down two cosmopolitans on her tray, he caught her gaze. Heat sizzled all the way down to her toes. Embarrassment be damned—she was hot for him and didn't seem to be able to help herself even if he was in complete control of himself. Control; right. She guessed his need to be in control extended to his libido, because once more, though she knew he'd been turned on as much as she, he'd ended the embrace before they could get carried away.

Carried away... That wasn't *her*.

How had this happened? she wondered. If ever

there was a mismatch waiting to happen, they were it.

"You need something else?"

Lynn blinked and looked down at the tray. He'd added a daiquiri, a beer and four Jell-O shots. "That's it," she said, a bit breathless.

At least that was it for the drinks. What she needed was, what? *Him?* In her life…in her bed…in her heart?

Or maybe he was already there, she thought recklessly, as she turned away from the bar and slowly made her way through the standing crowd toward the tables.

This didn't make any sense, and yet twice now she'd turned to Blade in distress. Any other man would have taken advantage of the situation, but not Blade. Was it really a control issue, though, or was he simply acting honorably?

Having hated her volatile home life while growing up, Lynn had always longed for a quiet, cultured man, one with whom she could share her love of the arts. Blade's idea of great art was probably a wall mural, his idea of great music undoubtedly a jam session on the streets. But she didn't care.

Blade could be volatile, too, being a product of an environment where he'd needed to prove himself, spending his young adulthood in the military. She always felt that possibility simmering under his quiet surface. On the other hand, he could be nurturing, she thought, as the music switched to something quieter, more haunting. "'Don't Turn Off the Lights' by Enrique Iglasias," the deejay announced.

That was it, she supposed. Vulnerable as she was, she couldn't resist what Blade offered. Though she'd never wanted to depend on anyone but herself, danger made her lose her perspective and respond instinctively.

After distributing the drinks and Jell-O shots, she took a food order from the next table, then went over to the computer and carefully entered each item. This part of the job wasn't as confusing as she'd feared it might be. The hardest part was being on her feet for so many hours. Too bad she'd never been into sensible shoes.

All her orders taken care of for the moment, she decided she needed a break. Todd, the waiter who'd showed her the ropes the day before, stopped next to her to use the computer.

"I need a break," she said. "Can you cover for me?"

"No problem."

The ladies' lounge was a haven, with comfortable upholstered chairs designed to give a girl relief from aching feet. When Lynn entered, Cass was freshening her makeup before a wall mirror, the frame of which was studded with fake gemstones in keeping with the club's jewel-tone decor.

"Hey, that audience loved you," Lynn said, plopping down in an emerald-green chair.

Cass fluffed a brush over her cheeks, then spun around on her stool. "They love being toyed with. That was an amateur's trick, and if they thought about it, they would get it," Cass admitted. "Unfortunately, I don't have a whole lot to work with."

"Self-taught?"

"Actually, I was once Max Street's assistant." Her expression darkened. "But that was in another lifetime."

"Maxwell Street?" Lynn had caught his television special the winter before. "His illusions are incredible. So you were in the big time…"

"And you're wondering how I landed here." Cass looked around the empty room as if wanting to make certain no one could overhear. "Unfortunately, I arrived here via prison, Lynn. I was convicted of making a valuable necklace disappear."

"I don't believe it. Your being a thief, that is."

"Thanks." Cass shrugged. "So, I did time for a theft I didn't commit. Someday I'll clear my name, though. I just haven't figured out how. But I have to do it. I have to be able to hold my head high again."

"You should hold your head high now," Lynn told her. A sharp study of character, no doubt due to her work, she heard the truth in Cass's words. "You know the truth even if the authorities don't."

"Yes, I do."

Because Cass seemed sad anyway, Lynn changed the subject. "So what other magic tricks can you do?"

"Illusions," Cass corrected. "They're not really tricks. You make the audience think they're seeing what they want to see, when all the time you have something else entirely up your sleeve."

"So *I'm* an illusion? Melinda Parker, that is?"

Cass laughed. "My finest work."

"So maybe I should think about doing more with that."

"Meaning?"

"I need resolution of my situation, Cass, whatever that takes."

"Lynn, be careful. Let the police do their job."

"The police have rules about how they conduct

themselves. Usually I do, too, since I'm an officer of the court. But in this case, I'm the victim, dammit! I don't want to play by the rules if that means I can't live my own life.''

''What does Blade think about this?''

''I haven't told him.'' Lynn shrugged. ''I'm sure he wouldn't approve.''

Lynn thought about that televised special and wondered how much Cass had picked up from her former employer. Maxwell Street had been able to hypnotize people, make them reveal information they'd claimed not to remember otherwise.

''Too bad you're not into hypnosis, too,'' she stated.

''Who needs to be hypnotized?''

''Me. I need my mind opened,'' she joked. ''Then maybe I could remember everything and put the guy who grabbed me behind bars before he can make good on his threats.''

''So you haven't remembered anything?''

''Bits and pieces. My brain is decidedly uncooperative.''

''Actually, I've tried my hand at hypnosis,'' Cass admitted.

Lynn started. ''Actually, I was kidding.''

''But it might be worth a try…''

Lynn's heart pounded faster at the thought. If it worked… But would it? She was used to having control over her own life, and so paranoid of letting anyone else in, the mere idea of being hypnotized choked her.

''You can trust me,'' Cass assured her.

But could she trust herself?

''Let me think about it.''

After the club closed and the rest of the staff went home, Lynn joined Cass and the men at the bar, where Gideon promptly gave Lynn the IDs he'd promised.

"I understand you had an incident this afternoon," he said.

Certain that he already had the details from Blade, she admitted, "A car chase. Rather, a car chasing my taxi. But I'm still in one piece."

"I already ran the plates as I'm sure the CPD did," Logan told her. "The car belongs to your parents' neighbor—well, someone who lives around the corner from them."

"You're sure?" Blade asked.

"It's official. The neighbor reported the car stolen late this afternoon."

"How?" Lynn remembered it being a new make. "It would have had a key with a computer chip—"

"An experienced thief can get any car," Blade told her.

"And in this case, the owner made it easy for the thief," Logan added. "He forgot something in the house and left the keys in the ignition. When he came out, the car was gone."

"Did anyone see anything?" Lynn asked.

Logan shook his head. "Sadly, no. They haven't found the vehicle yet, either, though if they ever do, it'll probably be clean of prints."

Disappointing news. Lynn had hoped the vehicle could be tracked to one of the suspects. So all she got out of the incident was proof that the villain was still after her and would use whatever means he needed to get to her.

"So, Lynn, the meeting is yours," Gideon said. "I

understand you have an idea of how to identify your abductor.''

She'd been thinking about that since having lunch with Stella. "First off, do you have access to a sound lab?''

"I might," Logan said.

"If we get recordings of all the suspect's voices, we could have an expert analyze them, see if one of them is a match to the message left at my office.''

"That might be doable," Logan said, "but it wouldn't be admissible in court.''

"Maybe not, but first things first. If we can identify the man…''

"That would be a step in the right direction," Gideon agreed.

Cass added, "Then we can figure out a way to nail him.''

"Whoa!" Blade said, the only negative voice in the room. "Let's not get ahead of ourselves.''

In the end, Logan set Lynn up in the club's security office with a recorder and computer software that would alter her own voice, and Blade agreed to bring her in the next afternoon to make the necessary calls.

"I have to get these recordings," she told him on the way home. "No matter how, even if I need to do it in person.''

"In person would be too dangerous," Blade objected.

Again the negativity.

"I'm safe enough in my new identity," Lynn insisted. "Those men would never recognize me, but I know who they are.''

"Wild talk. The police are on this. You'd be better to sit back and let them do their job.''

Lynn dropped the subject after that, but she couldn't stop thinking about it. Though she'd been in hiding only a few days, she was already feeling like a fugitive.

What if Stella and her colleagues didn't catch the villain? Lynn's life would never be normal or sane while a killer who wanted her dead was walking the streets. The longer it took, the more of an emotional mess she would be.

Not one for patience, Lynn knew she couldn't live this lie indefinitely.

ONCE MORE, Lynn had come to him for protection in the middle of the night. Not that she'd alerted him. She'd stolen silently through the bathroom and into his quarters, but still he'd been aware of her presence the moment she stepped foot in his room. He'd waited until she'd settled down on the couch, until her breathing had evened out and deepened. And then he'd left his bed to watch her sleep.

In the gym now, teaching her new self-defense techniques, Blade couldn't stop thinking about how scared she was and how brave and how foolish.

Wearing protection pads this morning, he said, "All right, mentally prepare yourself and get ready to do your worst."

Blade watched Lynn's features harden and her spine draw up straight as she walked by him across the mat. He waited only a second before lunging forward and grabbing her, pinning her arms to her sides. She was ready for him and drove her heel into his knee. Despite two-inch-thick leg padding, he felt the impact.

"Good!" he said, even as her foot continued a downward trajectory to stomp his toes. "Oww!"

"Omigod, I hurt you again!" Lynn turned in his arms, her lovely face filled with concern.

"Gotcha."

He watched the horror fade, replaced by indignation. "That wasn't funny."

"I kind of enjoyed it."

He was enjoying her. Enjoying watching her. Holding her.

"Don't do that to me. I still feel guilty about hitting you with that sculpture."

"Loosen up a little. The leg is fine, nearly good as new, and you're doing great. You're just so...intense."

"I want to get it right."

"And a fine job you're doing."

"Then maybe you could let go of me?"

As he released her, the flush in Lynn's cheeks told Blade she was as affected by being close as he was.

Not that he understood the attraction. They couldn't be more opposite. And she certainly wasn't his type. Normally he was drawn to women who were more open and honest about what they wanted. Women who would be glad to leave the tough stuff to him. Lynn was more of a mystery, one minute acting as if she didn't need him, the next as if she couldn't do without him.

But she sure had guts and wasn't about to back down from a challenge, not even one that had her scared to death. She wasn't a woman waiting to be rescued by a man. For that alone she had his respect, though he respected her in other ways, too.

Though a successful lawyer, Lynn seemed to put compassion before money. And her own safety. He thought about her insisting on dropping her disguise and going to court for Julie Wheeler. That said so much about her character. Lynn shouldered responsibility, more than she ought to…at least in the case of her sister's death.

"What next?" she asked, pulling him out of his musings.

"I'd try some frontal attacks on you, but these are the only eyes I have."

She gave him an arch expression. "You don't trust me?"

"I'm simply afraid you might get carried away with enthusiasm. You learn fast."

"Motivated is my middle name."

"Which one?"

Her forehead drawing into a frown, she echoed, "Which one what?"

"Evelyn Cross or Melinda Parker?"

"The *real* me."

"I'm not so sure anymore which one that is."

She grinned. "Thanks. I think."

"That was definitely a compliment. So let's try a couple more moves."

More relaxed than she had been the day before, Lynn got into the sparring with a visible enthusiasm. And Blade suspected it was more than her learning to protect herself. She was becoming comfortable with him. And she was letting down her guard.

Each time they made contact, his own pulse raced and his breathing quickened. He took every opportunity to touch her, to hold her. He couldn't get enough of her.

How would he ever let her go?

WALKING INTO THE CLUB'S security office midafternoon, Lynn was attacked by a surprising case of nerves. Stage fright? Maybe she should have asked Cass to do this. No doubt the other woman would have given the performance of a lifetime.

But it was important to Lynn that she take back her own life. She had to prove to herself that she wasn't helpless in the face of fear.

She set her file folder on the desk, saying, "I hope we can connect with the suspects at work."

"If we don't, we can always try later, at home," Blade said. "Or tomorrow."

Tomorrow... How many tomorrows would there be? It had only been a few days, but Lynn felt as if her life had been on hold forever.

Her only consolation was spending time with Blade. Once her abductor was identified and caught, she might never see him again—an unthinkable prospect, Lynn realized. In a few short days he'd become her anchor, her mentor, a vital part of her life.

"Let's set up the voice-alteration software first," Blade said, sitting down at the computer and bringing the program online.

He put on headsets and handed her a pair with an attached mike, and they did some testing. The end product was a slightly altered feminine voice that was higher and lighter than her own. Even so, butterflies attacked Lynn's stomach as she dialed the police station.

"Chicago Police Department, Area 3. Sergeant Thomas speaking."

"Detective Roger Wheeler, please."

"Hold on."

Hearing muffled voices in the background, Lynn licked her lips and tapped her nails against the desk.

And as she waited, she went over her cover story in her head. But when the sergeant came back to her it was with disappointing news.

"He's not in just now. Maybe in an hour."

Lynn hung up and in a whoosh let out the breath she hadn't even known she was holding. "No one home."

"You look a little pale," Blade said. "Are you sure you don't want me to do this?"

Lynn flushed. As always, he was considerate of her feelings. But this was one time he couldn't help her, other than taking charge of the equipment.

"I have to do something for myself," she insisted. "And I can handle Wheeler or anyone else. After all, it is at a distance."

"Just remember you're not alone in this."

He squeezed her hand, and the flush traveled through her to intimate spaces.

"I know I'm not alone and I appreciate that, Blade. But I've thought and thought about it, and I know I can't cower in a corner, waiting for fate to find me. It probably seemed like that's what I wanted a few days ago, but I was scared out of my mind. That's not really who I am."

"You don't have to tell me that. I know who you are."

For a moment, the connection between them was so strong it took her breath away. She'd never met a man like Blade Stone before. Or if she had, she'd been too blind to really see him. But her eyes were open now and she didn't intend to close them ever again.

Realizing he was staring at her, she cleared her

throat and mumbled, "Better get back to making calls before we run out of time."

Next she tried Victor Churchill, but his efficient secretary put her off, asking for her name and the number where she could be reached.

"Thanks, but I'll try again later." Lynn made a face, but before Blade could distract her again, immediately tapped in the next number. "If this one doesn't pan out, that'll make three strikes."

"But you won't give up," Blade said, sounding sure of himself. Rather, of her.

"No, I won't."

But three turned out to be the charm. Yes, Timothy Cooper was in, and yes, he would speak to her.

"Cooper."

"Mr. Cooper, this is Rachel Franklin."

"Yeah?"

"I'm with Sunshine Kitchens."

"Who?"

She met Blade's gaze and shrugged. Couldn't the man be polite enough to speak several words in a row? One-word sentences wouldn't help.

"We have a new line of spices and dressings and—"

"Nope."

"Surely there's something you need in the way of—"

"Yeah, for you to get off the phone so I can get back to work."

With that he hung up, leaving Lynn flushed with frustration. "Was that enough?" she asked Blade.

"We'll have to wait and see."

Nodding, she tapped in Johnny Rincon's number,

only to find it had been disconnected. She tried the operator and learned he had no telephone service.

"How can anyone not have a telephone?" she asked in wonder.

"Thank cell technology," Blade answered. "You can be sure he has one of those, even if it's in some-one else's name."

Which was why the operator couldn't find him in the system, Lynn thought. Trying Churchill again, she got the same song and dance from the secretary. So Lynn redialed the Area 3 station and asked to be put through to Wheeler. Three rings and the call went through.

"Violent Crimes."

In her softest, most ladylike voice she said, "De-tective Roger Wheeler, please."

"You got him."

Excited that at last she was having some luck, she gave Blade a thumbs up. "This is Rachel Franklin from the Lake Shore Ladies' League."

"What can I do for you, Miss Franklin?"

"That's Mrs."

"What can I do for you?" he repeated.

"Our league is very concerned with crime."

"You're reporting a crime?"

"We want to prevent one."

"I need *details.*"

"I'd like you to speak to our group about street safety."

"You what?" Wheeler sounded aggrieved. "I have cases to work. Call the community officer."

With that he hung up.

"Rude fellow," Blade said.

"I did get enough this time, right?"

"He said a whole lot more than your stalker did in the message we picked up at your office."

She breathed a sigh of relief. "Two down, two to go. Now if only I could get through to Victor Churchill. I wonder if that secretary of his ever takes a break."

"All you can do is keep trying."

So she tried again. No deal.

"Maybe there's another way to get to Churchill," she mused.

"And that would be?"

"Maria Savage is performing here Friday night," she said, thinking about using the local jazz singer's concert to her own advantage. "I've attended one of her performances. She's going big and the club will get plenty of press." Incentive for a man of some social standing to attend. "According to his ex-wife, Churchill likes showing his friends a good time. What if we messenger him an invitation for VIP seating, good for...say, six people?"

"You want to bring a potential criminal onto our turf?"

"That might be the only way I can get to him."

"He could be dangerous."

"He'll never recognize me."

"I thought you were comfortable at a distance."

"I changed my mind."

"You're not going anywhere near him."

Telling herself that Blade was merely showing his concern rather than being controlling, Lynn said, "Someone has to get close enough to get him on tape. I want to help nail him if he's guilty. Besides, no one really looks at their waitress."

"Unless the waitress looks like you do."

Smiling at Blade, Lynn circumvented his objection. "Then we're agreed?"

"Maybe Gideon won't agree—"

"So I'll foot the bill." She was trying not to get exasperated. "Now, what do we do about Johnny Rincon? I can't exactly call Carla and ask for her husband's cell phone number. If she even has it."

"Try Skipper's, a local bar. He hangs out there."

"You wouldn't have the number?" When he shrugged, she let directory assistance put her through.

"Skipper here."

"Of course you are," she said, making her voice flirty. "But is Johnny there?"

"Johnny who?"

She sighed heavily. "Who else? Johnny Rincon, of course."

"Nope. Ain't seen him today. If you want, you can leave a message."

"I'll try later, Skipper, sugar." She hung up and locked gazes with Blade. "This doesn't seem to be my day."

"Rincon'll show. Skipper's is his home away from home."

"Or...I could send *him* tickets to the performance, as well."

"Not a good idea."

Though a jolt of trepidation washed through her, she insisted, "I think it is."

"Johnny's dangerous."

"I want my life back. Besides, even if he does recognize me—which he won't—what can he do in a crowd?"

"What *can't* he do?" Blade countered. "We

haven't given the telephone a fair shot. Tomorrow afternoon you might get both Churchill and Rincon.''

''What if I don't?''

His expression darkened and his jaw visibly clenched. ''You still need to rethink the whole concert idea.''

It was clear exactly how dangerous he thought Rincon might be. Lynn felt a shiver of apprehension and suddenly got cold feet.

''All right, I'll think about it,'' she agreed.

Knowing that, in the end, she would do whatever she must to take back her life.

Chapter Nine

As he mixed drinks that night, Blade tried to believe that Lynn would listen to him about Johnny Rincon. She didn't know who she was dealing with when it came to that scum.

Too bad she couldn't have reached him by telephone, because then maybe they could be sure about him one way or the other. They'd given the tape with Cooper's and Wheeler's recorded voices to Logan, who'd said he'd have an answer about them sometime the next day.

All of which reminded Blade that he hadn't gotten back to Leroy, so on his first break, he made for the security office and used Logan's phone. Unfortunately, the man wasn't home, so he called Skipper's again and gave the owner his story about needing to speak to Leroy about a car.

And when Leroy got on the phone, he played right along. "I might have a lead on that Corvette you wanted. It's a little shaky, though."

Blade knew the man had to be cautious about what he said in the likely event that someone would report anything suspicious back to Johnny. Blade noted the way the background sound had dropped, as if every ear in the bar was attuned to Leroy's conversation.

"So you spoke to someone who knows where Johnny was last weekend?" he asked.

Leroy laughed. "Yeah, I know, a Corvette's slung low and rides fast...kinda like a woman."

"You're saying Johnny was with a woman?"

"That's what I hear."

"Then you couldn't confirm that?"

"Afraid not. I couldn't get those specifications."

Reading between the lines, Blade said, "So no one actually saw Johnny around with this woman last weekend. Supposedly he was holed up somewhere doing the horizontal mambo."

"That's exactly right. I'm not really sure about this one, though. But I'll keep checking on it if you're still interested."

Not wanting Leroy to court any more trouble, Blade said, "Drop it. You've done enough."

"Well, if you're sure I can't interest you... Good luck elsewhere, then."

His mood darker than before, Blade made his way back to the bar only to find Stella Jacobek there, waiting for him. He poured her a beer and set it on the bar before her, just as Lynn joined them.

"How is the investigation going?" she asked the detective.

"The team has run through the list of suspects and we were able to catch up with all but the guy who went out of the country. I can't say I'm impressed with any of these jerks. But they all have alibis."

"Including Johnny?" Blade asked, watching for Lynn's reaction.

But when Stella said, "*Especially* Johnny," Lynn's reaction was neutral.

Whatever she was thinking, she was keeping it to herself.

Stella added, "Three of his boys say they were in an all-night poker game on Saturday."

Blade shook his head. "Not according to Leroy."

"Leroy? You involved Leroy? You know how many mouths that guy's feeding?"

"I told him to drop it. But according to him the word is Johnny was holed up with a new squeeze all weekend. And yet no one saw him with or without a woman."

"Well, well, well." Stella grinned at him. "This may be the nail in Johnny Rincon's coffin, at last."

"Wait," Lynn said. "So you think he's the one?"

"Unless he comes up with an alibi—"

"Listen, Star," Blade interrupted, "Johnny is more dangerous than ever. Let someone else handle—"

"Whoa, no lectures, Blade."

"He's good at that," Lynn said.

Stella's smile was gone, replaced by a tough visage. "I'm not Star anymore. I'm not a kid. And you're talking about my job here. I've been wanting to nail that bastard on something for a long, long time."

Even though he knew she was right, Blade felt his gut tighten at the thought of her confronting their old nemesis head-on. "Just don't tell me not to worry. And promise me you won't do anything without backup."

"Deal."

His old friend's agreement made Blade feel better. He and Lynn told her about their afternoon recording session—off the record and without involving Logan. Lynn offhandedly said she'd found the recording setup in a shop down the street, and Blade was happy to see that she was keeping the team's existence under wraps.

When he announced that Lynn planned on going to court the next day, Stella promised to see what she could do to alert security in the Daley Building.

A guy at a nearby table waved frantically for attention, and Lynn went off to get his order, leaving Blade alone with Stella.

"So what's new with you?" he asked.

She grinned. "How can you tell?"

"Well, I couldn't, but I can now. What's his name?"

"Hugh Keaton."

"He must be treating you right."

"We just ran into each other earlier today. Literally," she added. "Outside the cop shop. And as a matter of fact, I'm going to meet him now. We have a late date."

Blade arched a brow. "Don't do anything I wouldn't do."

Stella's smile widened as she slipped off her stool. "That leaves a lot of wiggle room."

"You can tell me just how much tomorrow."

ON HER BREAK, Lynn decided to make some calls, and Gideon told her to go ahead and use the telephone in his office.

She made herself comfortable at the desk, which included slipping off her high-heeled sandals. A shoe maven, she had to admit her collection wasn't meant for waitressing, and she had a moment's regret that she hadn't gone out and bought something sensible. Rubbing a sore spot with one hand, she used the other to call her office number again.

No whispered messages.

Relieved, she placed a call to Julie Wheeler and reconfirmed the next day's court date, reassuring the nervous woman that she would be there and fighting for her one hundred percent.

Then she switched feet and phone numbers, this time calling home to pick up her messages. Her girlfriends had somehow found out about her ordeal and had called from Hawaii expressing their concern, but they hadn't left a number where they could be reached.

And her stalker seemed oddly silent.

She should be happy…so why did the fact make her uncomfortable?

What was he up to?

Trying to put her own situation out of mind, she dialed her parents' number. As always, her mother answered.

"Hey, Mom, how is it going?"

"Everything is fine, honey."

That her mother didn't sound fine immediately put Lynn on edge. "What's wrong?"

"Nothing."

"Mom…"

"Nathan is here."

"Again?" Lynn didn't have to ask why. "You haven't given him Dani's address or phone number, have you?"

"Well, not exactly."

Which meant she'd given him something. "But you told him she's in London, right?"

"Yes."

"Don't tell him anything more, Mom, please—not until I can speak to Dani myself, make sure she wants Nathan to be able to find her." When her mother didn't answer, Lynn closed her eyes. "Let me speak to Nathan."

"All right."

She heard her mother call him to the phone. Trying not to let herself get upset, Lynn flexed her ankles and toes and thought about soaking her feet when she got home.

Then Nathan said, "Evelyn."

She was glad to hear caution in his voice. "Nathan. I wanted you to know that I thought about our conversation…"

Voice tight, he said, "And?"

"And I decided that I would call Dani and talk to her for you."

He laughed and sounded relieved. "Hey, you won't be sorry, I promise."

"But whether or not she wants to talk to you is up to her."

"I get that."

"So in the meantime, I would appreciate it if you didn't press my parents for information. It's not fair to them."

She was met with silence.

"Nathan?"

"Yeah, okay, I'll back off," he agreed.

But she could tell he wasn't happy about it. She supposed he was simply anxious.

"So when are you going to call Danielle?"

She checked her watch. It was past midnight London time, but her sister had always been a late night person. When she did go to bed, she always turned off her phone and let voice mail pick up.

"I'll call tonight, but I'll probably have to leave a message."

"Great. Thank you. I know if you tell her how hard I'm working to get her back, she'll want to hear from me."

Actually, Lynn didn't really know, since she hadn't spoken to his therapist. And at the moment, the idea of doing so was out of the question.

"I'm not making any promises."

"Right. It's up to Danielle. I get that."

"Good. Let me speak to Mom again."

"Mother Cross…"

Slipping her shoes back on, Lynn winced but somehow convinced herself her feet felt a bit better.

A moment later, her mother came back on the line. Lynn asked about her father, then once again pleaded with her mom to keep Dani's council.

True to her promise, Lynn then tried Dani, charging the call to her own phone. But the voice mail was turned on, so she left a message, telling her sister all about her conversation with Nathan.

And before she hung up, she added, "Listen, Dani, I've been thinking that maybe I got a little too involved in your marriage. Maybe gave you some bad advice. I probably should have stayed out of it. I'm really sorry…."

With that she hung up, her hand trembling on the receiver.

"Bad news?"

She whipped around. "Blade. I didn't hear you come in."

"What's wrong?"

"Nothing to do with my abduction," she was quick to assure him. "Family stuff."

"I'm a good listener."

"Thanks."

But she didn't particularly want to admit her feeling of culpability in her sister's divorce. That would bring up a whole can of worms that she would rather keep buried.

Luckily, the phone rang. "Maybe you ought to get that."

Blade picked up. "Club Undercover." He listened for a moment, then gave the caller directions.

Giving Lynn a chance to escape without having to answer more questions.

BLADE COULDN'T HELP wondering what was bothering Lynn. But since it was a family matter, which he equated with private, he chose not to press her.

Not that he had a chance at work, anyway.

The club was full, the dance floor packed with bodies gyrating to the music and the giant video images on the wall screen behind them. The drinks were flowing, not only from the main bar but from the VIP bar up at street level. Customers were coming from all over the city, and the suburbs as well, to check out Club Undercover. Having seen the steady rise in business over the last several months, Blade knew that Gideon had a huge hit on his hands.

So it was no wonder that when they left the club in the wee hours, Lynn seemed exhausted and barely able to walk.

"You're limping."

"These shoes weren't made for walking. At least not waitressing. I think my blisters have blisters."

"Maybe a trip to a shoe store is in order."

Lynn simply groaned and stopped a moment to slip them off her feet. With what sounded like a relieved sigh, she walked the rest of the way to the car barefoot.

When they got home, Blade immediately drew a tub of water and told Lynn to soak as long as she liked and to let him know when she was done.

"And let me know if you need your back scrubbed," he added through the door.

Her answer was another groan and a splash as she slid into the tub.

For a moment, he imagined her soaping up, with him there to do her back…leading to other, more intimate touching….

That's where he put a hold on his imagination— where the name Cross lit up his mind. Where the image of a woman dead, killed by him, took over.

He could still see her slender body, facedown in the street, blond hair hiding her features.

He'd known then, at that exact moment, what a mistake he'd made. A moment frozen in time for him, as fresh in his mind as if it had just happened. A moment that might have gotten him killed if one of his buddies hadn't tackled him. As it was, he'd already been wounded, the reason he'd spun around, gun firing when he'd heard a sound behind him, only to hit an innocent woman who'd walked in on the raid….

He'd spent weeks in recovery. Weeks with nothing to do but think, while the authorities covered up the carefully planned Black Ops mission gone bad. Weeks with guilt eating at him until he knew he couldn't go on, could no longer work in Special

Forces, couldn't think about ever again hurting an innocent person.

His military career had been over.

And nothing had ameliorated the guilt. Not until now…maybe…if he could keep Lynn safe.

The bathroom door opening brought him back to the present.

"I'm done," she said, poking her head out. "Did you want me to start water for you?"

He blinked at her and for a moment saw her sister. Then he shook away the image and said, "Thanks, no. How are the feet?"

"A little better."

"Come on in here and I'll work on them."

"A foot rub?"

She sounded simultaneously cautious and pleased.

"I have some salve here guaranteed to cure what ails you."

Still a bit tentative, she came into his quarters dressed in a nightshirt that stopped right above her knees. The soft material clung to her curves and all the damp spots she hadn't toweled dry.

Mouth going dry, he averted his eyes and said, "Sit."

"Where?"

"Couch."

After fetching the salve from the bathroom, he sat next to her and indicated she should swing up her legs. He placed her feet in his lap. Then he opened the jar and released the scent of wildflowers. He slathered the cool paste onto one foot, then the other. She was looking with curiosity at the jar in his hand.

"No label," she said. "What is it?"

"Something my Iroquois grandfather taught me to

make when we went on a quest together.'' He smoothed the salve over the top of her left foot. ''We walked for a week, and the only way I got through it was to use his special concoction.''

After her toes, he massaged the ball of her foot and worked his way down to the heel. Her foot quivered under his ministrations and he was hard-pressed to keep his mind on what he was doing rather than on what he would like to do.

Lynn sighed. ''If I can walk pain-free, I'm going to start calling you Mr. Folk Medicine.''

''It works,'' he assured her, his voice tight from the contact. Against his will, he wanted to work his way back up, past her ankle, around her calf, over her knee.... ''We can't have you limping to court tomorrow.''

He started on her right foot.

Groaning with obvious pleasure, she said, ''It's not court I'm worried about.''

''You *should* be worried.''

''I have you to worry for me,'' she murmured, her eyes fluttering closed. ''And to guard my body.''

He wanted to do a lot more to her body than guard it. He wanted to touch every inch of it, starting with those long legs and working his way up to her hips.

His turn to groan. There was no reaction from Lynn, thankfully.

She was asleep.

''*...POISON TO A RELATIONSHIP...*''

Lynn stirred and protested halfheartedly.

''*...don't know what it's like...never a man of your own...*''

In the half sleep of dawn, Lynn faced her abductor,

but his features were a blur. She was dream-
ing…awakening…fighting to go down deeper.

"*…deserve to die…*"

His whisper echoed as she came fully awake with
a gasp.

It took her a moment to orient herself.

Gray light spilled through the windows, casting
deep shadows around the room.

Blade's room.

Though he'd left her on the couch, he'd placed a
pillow under her head and had covered her with a
sheet.

He'd taken care of her. Again.

Rising so as not to waken him, she slipped into the
bathroom. And as she closed the door again, she
heard a final whisper in her head.

"*Until we meet again…*"

Chapter Ten

Lynn had never been this nervous going to court since her first case. She was wearing her own clothes and had washed the blue streaks out of her hair, then had bound it back from her face, the way she usually wore it to court. Somehow she still looked different, and not because of the lighter shade of blond, which was hardly apparent in this style.

So what was it? she wondered.

Though she'd always thought of herself as a woman of substance, being abducted had shaken her confidence. But now her determination was renewed, Lynn thought gratefully, and she had Team Undercover to thank for that. Especially Blade.

"Ready?" he asked, flicking his gaze over her lawyerly outfit.

Whether or not he approved, she couldn't tell. She certainly approved of him. He was wearing tan slacks and a camel jacket. His cream shirt lay open at the throat, revealing lightly bronzed skin and the leather pouch he always wore. If she'd found him handsome before, he appeared stunning to her now. He was a beautiful man, she admitted, both outside and in.

A little breathless, she said, "Ready or not..."

He held the door for her and placed a hand in the middle of her back as though he were her escort rather than her bodyguard. Almost as though they were on a date.

Her throat closed as she thought about it. About him. About them together.

What was going on with her? She'd never obsessed over a man, not even ones with whom she'd slept.

A thought that opened a can of worms for her.

She'd been perfectly willing to sleep with Blade that first night, her attempt to make herself feel better. He hadn't been willing to sleep with her. And yet she knew he was attracted to her. She saw the way he looked at her at times, the smoldering glance of a man who was imagining pleasuring her....

She tightened her thighs as liquid pooled from her center. Sliding into the Jeep's passenger seat only intensified the sensation, especially when he got in beside her.

Giving Blade a quick glance—no, he couldn't tell how perturbed she was—Lynn tried to get her mind off him and impossibilities.

Once on their way, she said, "Security is tight at the Daley Center."

"Good."

She was remembering the knife she'd seen strapped to his leg when she said, "I was actually thinking about the metal detector."

"Don't worry, I won't hold you up."

So he wasn't wearing a weapon—not that it bothered her. Lynn was certain Blade could take care of her just fine without external aid.

"Being held up isn't what worries me," she said. "I just don't want to be the cause of any trouble for you. Rather, any more trouble,'' she amended, thinking of how she'd disrupted his life.

''You're no trouble. And I'm glad to do it.''

''For Stella?''

''For Evelyn Cross.''

What an odd answer, she thought. Not for *you* but for *Evelyn Cross*. As though he was speaking of a person who wasn't there. As if her name was more important than she herself was. He probably meant the public persona, the lawyer who aided the defenseless even if they didn't have money. He hadn't told her much about his mother and sister, so for all she knew, he was relating to something that had happened to one of them.

Though she couldn't explain why, somehow his protecting her felt personal. Personal to him, that was. Odd. She didn't feel like questioning him about it.

Nor did she feel like thinking too far into the future, even though, more and more, she wondered if it really mattered that they had only a shared need for justice.

Could that possibly be enough on which to build a relationship?

It seemed not, and yet she felt so lost every time she thought about her abductor being caught and put behind bars. Then she and Blade would have no reason to continue seeing each other. It bothered Lynn that she couldn't even fathom life without him.

Breaking into her thoughts, he said, ''Stella set up a uniform to keep an eye on Wheeler's movements at the Daley Center. But, considering Wheeler's a detective with the Chicago Police Department, he'll be watched from a discreet distance.''

''Then all my bases are covered.''

For some reason, Lynn would put more trust in Blade himself than in some cop she'd never met.

A short while later, they'd parked the Jeep and were crossing Daley Plaza on foot when a familiar figure disengaged himself from the gigantic metal Picasso sculpture—where he'd been talking to another man—just as if he'd been waiting for her arrival. His silver hair seemed to bristle as he marched toward her. He might be older than the other suspects, but as always, he appeared to be as fit as a thirty-year-old.

"That's Victor Churchill," she murmured, and felt Blade's arm go around her.

As he got within earshot, Churchill said, "Imagine you showing your face in public, Evelyn."

"You have a problem with that?" she retorted. Blade gave her an encouraging squeeze.

"New boy toy?" Churchill asked with a sneer. "Bad choice. This one's not going to get you into the North Shore Yacht Club."

Though she was insulted for Blaze, Lynn snapped, "I can get myself there if I so desire."

Churchill laughed. "You'd do that, wouldn't you? Put yourself on display, give the guy who gave you what for the finger."

"Excuse me?"

"The guy who kidnapped you. He did the men of this city a service trying to take you out. I would shake his hand if I could, Evelyn. And then I would ask him why he didn't finish the job."

Laughing, Churchill moved off. And a distraught Lynn stood there gaping, then caught at Blade's arm as he seemed about to go after the bastard. One look at her and he froze, but she could see concern hardening his features.

Knowing she had to get herself in the right frame of mind for court, Lynn tried to make light of the incident. "And I was worried about Wheeler... But Churchill's probably all talk. A man like that wouldn't really get his hands dirty."

"He could pay someone else to get what he wanted."

She shook her head. "No. It was personal. The man who grabbed me wasn't doing someone else's dirty work." Though she didn't remember much, the pure animosity of her captor hadn't escaped her.

Getting through Daley Center security went smoothly, and Lynn led the way to the correct bank of elevators and up to the scheduled divorce court. Julie Wheeler was already waiting in the hallway, and her soon-to-be ex-husband seemed to have her cornered. Heart thumping at the prospect of having a face-to-face with another suspect on the heels of her encounter with Churchill, Lynn tried to push away the fear as she went straight up to him.

"There's a restraining order charging you to stay away from your wife, Mr. Wheeler."

He whirled on her so fast that her heart jumped. Sparks seemed to fly from his eyes. "You know what you can do with your court order!" he snarled.

"Perhaps you should tell that to the judge and get his opinion—"

"Bitch!"

Hands balled into fists, Wheeler stepped toward Lynn threateningly, and her heart raced right up into her throat. But before she had a chance to move away, Blade stepped between them.

"Who the hell are you?" Wheeler rasped.

"If you touch either of these women, I'll be your worst nightmare."

"Your name!" Wheeler demanded.

"Blade. And I can be as deadly as that sounds."

"Are you threatening me?"

"Do you need to be threatened?" Blade asked quietly. "Because I can be more specific. I can elaborate on how I spent nearly a decade in—"

Lynn gripped his arm and stopped him from going on. "Don't test that court order again," she snapped at Wheeler, "or I'll have you arrested."

The man's eyes blazed with hatred. But apparently Blade's presence kept him from issuing a direct threat. Or maybe it was his lawyer rushing to intercept him, a frantic expression on his jowly face.

"Thank you, Evelyn," Julie said as her husband was pulled away by his lawyer. "Don't let your guard down, though. It's easy to see how much Roger hates you, and he doesn't let hate go easily."

"It doesn't seem that he treats people differently if he hates them or loves them. I'll see what I can do about making sure he gets counseling."

"It won't do any good," Julie said, shaking her head. "Nothing will."

Lynn remembered Julie telling her that her husband had been put in an anger management program by the department, but that he had made it look good, while flipping off the therapist behind his back.

Considering his position in the Chicago Police Department, Wheeler's disregard for authority was especially concerning. And yes, he'd beaten offenders and bragged about it, and he'd threatened his wife with the same, had bullied her and their kids into submission for years.

But did that make him a potential killer? Did that make him a man who would abduct a woman and torture her by issuing death threats? Lynn simply didn't know.

She refused to let her indecision about Wheeler's innocence or guilt affect her court performance, however. And in the end, she got what Julie wanted in the custody agreement, at least on the surface. Roger Wheeler would not be able to see his children unless he agreed to counseling, and only after the therapist decided his children would be safe could the custody issue be revisited.

"I don't know how to thank you," Julie said afterward.

"Just take care of yourself. Stay safe."

Eyes averted, Julie mumbled, "You, too," as she walked away.

Making Lynn wonder again about Roger Wheeler. Did his now-ex-wife believe that he was the offender in her case?

"Good job," Blade said.

"I hope so. And I hope Wheeler's not the one. If he could abduct me and threaten me with death, what might he do to the woman who spurned him?"

A chill shot through her and she shuddered. Blade lightly wrapped an arm around her back. The warmth of his palm breached the thin material of her suit jacket. With him at her side, she felt safe.

As they walked through the halls, lawyers she knew greeted her, a few women giving Blade a thorough once-over and her a look of envy. Biting back a smile, Lynn couldn't help herself—she moved possessively closer.

They had just skated around a janitor mopping the

floor when suddenly an attractive redhead flew at them and grabbed Blade's lapels.

"My little girl," the woman gasped. "She's only seven and she wandered off. Have you seen her?"

"Sorry, can't say that I have."

"I only turned away for a moment!"

He looked around. "You'd better find security—"

The stranger tugged at his lapels. "Help me, please!"

Blade gave Lynn a what-do-I-do-now expression.

"Help her find security," Lynn said. "It'll only take a minute. I'll be in there." She indicated the nearby ladies' room.

Though he didn't look happy, Blade nodded and led the woman in the other direction.

Lynn headed for the rest room, only to see a Closed for Cleaning sign. As she started to turn away, a push from behind shoved her straight inside.

"Hey!"

She caught herself against a wall and started to turn back, but whoever had pushed her was there, pressing up against her.

A man.

Then the truth came to her, made her lose her breath, when he whispered into her ear, "You should stay out of other peoples' lives, Evelyn. Interfering isn't healthy."

Lynn froze, and what felt like a brick in her throat made it impossible to say anything, impossible to breathe. This couldn't be happening to her, not again, not in a public place. Not when she had a bodyguard....

A bodyguard who'd conveniently been distracted.

Another woman had helped this bastard get to her?

Outraged, Lynn came to life, trying to swing, but the villain had one hand tangled in her hair and the other around her body so that she couldn't move...couldn't see what he looked like.

A choked sound barely left her mouth before a rag shoved into her face cut off the rest of the scream.

"...you need to be taught a lesson, Evelyn..."

Lynn swayed as the memory fragment tangled with the present. Her head was already growing light. Knowing she would be unconscious in seconds if she didn't fight it, she held her breath against the fumes and tried to rip her head away. Still he held her fast, a steely arm around her body, pinning her elbows to her sides as he shoved her forward.

Acting on instinct, she kicked backward as Blade had taught her, but her balance was shaky, and her heel slid off his shin instead of making contact with his knee. While he grunted, the kick didn't stop him.

Before she could regroup, she had to gasp for air, and her head grew even lighter.

"...you destroyed my world...."

Another fragmented memory...

Again she held her breath as her abductor propelled her forward. Her flailing feet kicked the Closed sign, sending it skittering against the wall as the bastard forced her farther into the empty rest room.

Removing the rag from her mouth and nose, he whispered, "I don't want you unconscious, Evelyn. I want you to know exactly what's happening to you."

He shoved her into a stall and down hard onto her knees. Sharp pain made her cry out. That and the toilet bowl looming closer.

"I want you to know what it feels like to die, Eve-

lyn,'' he whispered, ''and know that no one and nothing can save you this time.''

''What...?'' she mumbled, and then thought feign-
ing unconsciousness might be her best choice.

She let her weight drop back against him, but he
wasn't fooled. He renewed his tight grip on her hair
and shoved her face forward and down so that she
was faced with the bowl of water and realized he
meant to drown her in it.

Whoever he was...

Roger Wheeler seeking instant retribution?

''No!'' she cried weakly.

On her knees with him pressed up behind her, she
was helpless to use any of the techniques Blade had
taught her. She struggled and turned her head, felt
water slap against the side of her face.

''Don't bother fighting it.'' He released pressure
for just a second, and she sucked in air and a whiff
of toilet bowl cleaner. ''You can't hold your breath
long enough.''

And while holding her breath she couldn't scream,
Lynn thought as the water rushed up at her. But what
choice did she have?

She closed her eyes tight and resisted all she could.
Fought the gag reflex that threatened her even though
the bowl had been newly cleaned. She reached back
with one hand, searching for a hold as he pushed her
head down into the water. Finding purchase on the
soft flesh of his inner thigh with her fingers, she
pinched him as hard as she could while water covered
her forehead, her closed eyes, her nose....

When she heard a scream, she imagined it was her
own voice echoing through her mind.

But suddenly the bastard released her and flew

back. She pulled herself free of the toilet bowl with
a gasp and a spray of water.

Another scream—not his, but a woman's!

Gagging and wiping at her tightly closed eyes with
her jacket sleeve, Lynn shoved herself out of the stall.
She opened them just in time to see the back of a
janitor's uniform as the bastard fled out the far door.

The woman who'd screamed rushed at her. "I
didn't know. Honest!" she cried. "Are you okay?"

The redhead who'd distracted Blade, a horrified
Lynn realized.

Then suddenly Blade was there in person.

Before he could help her up to her feet, Lynn
gasped, "Go! That way!" and pointed to the door on
the other hall. She could take care of the redhead.
Even as she added, "Janitor's uniform," he was gone.

Chapter Eleven

Fighting his instinct to stop and wrap Lynn in his arms and make certain she was unharmed, Blade shot after the man who'd taken her, and on *his* watch.

Another mistake.

How many could he make?

Thank God the bastard hadn't killed her.

Blade flew into the corridor and looked around. Dozens of people milled about him. There was no sign of a man in a janitor's uniform, but he spotted a cop.

Rushing toward him, Blade said, "Ladies' room. A woman was attacked."

Even as the cop raced toward the rest room, Blade plowed through the crowd, head turning, gaze searching, but not finding the one thing he sought. He stopped and changed tactics. Turned in a circle.

All to no avail.

"Janitor!" he yelled, as though he were crying fire. "Anyone seen a janitor?"

Most people ignored him, a few gave him odd looks, but one elderly woman said, "There." She nodded toward the emergency stairs.

"Thanks."

He rushed into the stairwell, mind racing. Up or down? How many floors?

Stopping, he closed his eyes and focused inward as first his Iroquois grandfather and then his Special Forces training had taught him to do. The slight scrape of a leather sole against cement whispered up to him from below.

Then Blade was off, taking two stairs at a time, using the railing to launch himself around corners, and jumping down to landings.

When he caught up to the bastard, he'd have to control himself so that he didn't break his damn neck for abusing Lynn. He could almost see his prey now; glimpses of gray uniform assured him he was gaining on the bastard.

Only two floors separating them...one and a half...one...

Lynn's attacker moved fast.

Blade moved faster.

With only a handful of stairs between them, he launched himself at his prey's back and brought him down hard, facedown. Now he had the bastard! But as Blade grasped his shoulder to spin him around, the man tore a bottle from his uniform and sprayed.

Liquid flooded Blade's eyes and made him cry out. When he threw up his hands as though he could stop the burn, the villain shoved an elbow into his gut and propelled him to the side. Blade fell back, smacking the healing cut on his calf against a stair. Catching himself, he tried to open his eyes and focus, to no avail. He barely caught sight of a gray uniform before squeezing his lids tight again.

The bastard's laugh was followed by the snick of a door opening and closing.

Blindly trying to follow, Blade cursed long and loud.

Once more, the villain had escaped.

"YOU'RE LUCKY he didn't blind you permanently," Stella told Blade after they'd settled into a conference room to go over the details of the attack. "You should have let him go, and stayed with Lynn. That was the agreement."

"I had him," Blade growled, sounding as disgusted and frustrated as Lynn was feeling.

They'd been prepared, but her abductor had gotten to her again, anyway. They'd both had physical contact and yet neither had seen his face.

Now Blade was looking at her with a sorrowful expression. Lynn knew he felt guilty because he thought he'd let her down. But he hadn't.

She swallowed hard. Despite Blade's immediately flushing of his eyes with cool water, they looked alarmingly red to her. The paramedic who'd checked him had applied some kind of drops and said he'd be okay. She'd been checked over, too, though all she'd needed was to wash her wet hair and skin with antibacterial soap. Just thinking about having her head shoved into a toilet creeped her out.

Stella settled her rear at the edge of a desk and said, "Ms. Tara Crane claims some guy she didn't know paid her fifty dollars to play a prank on a friend."

"I believe her," Lynn said. "She did scream for help. She seemed freaked. And sorry."

Though Lynn didn't know if she could forgive the young woman, she didn't want Tara Crane to be another victim of the bastard who'd almost killed *her*.

"Unfortunately, Ms. Crane's description isn't much better than yours."

"*What* description?" Lynn asked, disgusted that she hadn't gotten so much as a glimpse of the man's face.

"Exactly. Your attacker wore a billed cap and sunglasses with the janitor's uniform when he approached her. He kept his head down and his voice low, revealing no distinguishing accent or phraseology."

"Well, it couldn't have been Roger Wheeler, right?" Lynn asked. "Since you had a uniform tailing him."

"About that…" Stella cleared her throat and pulled the pencil free of the twist of hair at the nape of her neck. "It seems the officer got distracted and lost him within minutes of your leaving the courtroom."

The information was like a splash of cold water in the face. "Then he could be the one."

"I'm afraid so."

"Or Victor Churchill," Blade mused.

"How's that?" Stella asked.

"He was here today," Lynn said, remembering the man's animosity toward her. She told Stella all about the "chance" meeting. "But Wheeler's got to be the one. It all fits."

Stella didn't take her up on that. Instead, she said, "I wonder what our other boys were doing at the time. If we could actually place Rincon or Cooper for sure, that might eliminate a suspect or two."

"Leroy might be able to place Johnny," Blade mused. "Don't worry, I'll tell him to keep a low profile on this."

Stella nodded. "And I'll see what our macabre chef

was up to, plus try to get a handle on Wheeler's and Churchill's whereabouts.''

Knowing alibis could be just that, Lynn held her own council, while deciding to go ahead with plans of her own.

HOURS LATER, Blade still cursed the fact that not only had he been caught off guard, he'd been taken down by an amateur with a bottle of spray cleaner. The club hadn't opened yet, and he and Lynn sat at a table in the employees lounge, waiting for the other members of Team Undercover to join them for an update.

Lynn looked like hell. Not that she wasn't still beautiful, no doubt about it. But he'd come to know her body language, her every expression. And before him sat a woman on edge, one who'd been through the wringer.

And it was all his fault.

''I can't believe I let the bastard get to you.''

''Enough apologizing already,'' she replied.

''But I left you and—''

''And nature was calling me. You couldn't have held my hand in the ladies' room.''

''But I should have been guarding the door.''

''There was *another* door,'' she reminded him, as Cass entered the lounge. ''Or I should have gone with you. We can play this blame game as long as you like, but it isn't going to change the outcome. The crux of the matter is that I'm all right. It's time to get on with things.''

Suspicion tickled the back of his neck. ''What things?''

Lynn didn't answer, merely looked to the doorway as Gideon entered, followed by Logan.

Though the team members already knew about the latest attack, Lynn gave them all the gory details. And made Blade want to kick himself to kingdom come all over again.

"Looks like you need to stick to your new identity until we get a break," Gideon said.

"Too bad you can't remember the *details* of the original situation." Cass sat and met Lynn's gaze as if she were trying to mesmerize her. "You *really* ought to consider *jogging* that *memory.*"

Blade wondered what Cass was getting at, especially when, as if she were stricken with a case of nerves, Lynn quickly looked away from the other woman.

Did Cass know something he didn't?

Trying not to let it worry him, Blade told Logan, "We tried again to get Churchill and Johnny on tape this afternoon, but no luck."

"Too bad. At least I got results on the other two back from the lab."

Lynn visibly perked up. "And?"

"And we can eliminate one of the suspects."

"Timothy Cooper," Blade guessed.

"Actually, Roger Wheeler."

"What?" Lynn gasped. "Are you sure?"

Though Blade hadn't seen the bastard's face, they'd made physical contact. From the man's wiliness and strength, he would have gone with the younger, more street savvy cop than a businessman.

Then again, Johnny was street-smart and tough as they came...although how the hell would he have known where to find Lynn that morning?

"No room for doubt?" Blade asked.

"Not if you believe voice analysis has basis

in fact,'' Logan said. ''The speech patterns, the breathing...well, they indicate Wheeler to be improbable, while Cooper is labeled neutral due to lack of sufficient material.''

''I was so sure,'' Lynn murmured. ''Everything fit. I mean, Wheeler was right there, in my face. He threatened me less than an hour before it happened!''

''As did Churchill,'' Blade reminded her.

''Right.''

She didn't sound any more convinced than he was, Blade realized.

Churchill *could* have done it. Stella had checked him out. He'd had business at the Daley Center that morning. But the man couldn't come up with anyone to corroborate where he'd been at the time of the attack. Of course, he'd had an important meeting a half hour following, and according to Churchill's colleagues, he'd shown up on time.

Could he have played it so close to the wire? Blade wondered.

''Maybe we need to put tails on the three remaining suspects,'' Gideon said.

''Twenty-four-seven?'' Blade asked.

''That's probably the only way—''

''No!'' Lynn slammed down her cup of coffee and sloshed some on her hand. ''What good would that do unless I gave the creep another shot at Evelyn Cross? I don't think so. I want to play this *my* way.''

Knowing what she meant by that, Blade felt his gut knot. He glared at Lynn, but she refused to meet his gaze. Color heightened her cheeks and that wounded, trapped expression had left her features. Which was good, he guessed. She was ready to fight back.

Suddenly he realized that Gideon, Logan and Cass were all staring at the two of them, waiting....

And then Gideon broke the tension by clearing his throat. "What would your way be, Lynn?"

"Since we couldn't get all the suspects' voices on tape, I figured that if I sent out some VIP tickets for the Maria Savage concert tomorrow night, it might give me the opportunity to get up close and personal. I could wear a wire while serving drinks."

Back to that again—Blade knew it!

His throat went tight when he asked, "You're talking about Churchill, right?"

"Uh-huh. And Cooper."

But he could hear the addendum in her tone. And she still refused to look at him.

"Leave Johnny alone," he ordered, his voice low and far more calm than he was feeling.

Lynn tightened her jaw at his warning and didn't answer one way or another. No one in the room said a thing, and he could almost hear the others' thoughts. It might be the only way. And the team would all be there to back her up.

That didn't mean Blade had to like it, of course...or give his approval. He knew Lynn well enough to be convinced she would do what she wanted, anyway.

"It's time to get to work," Gideon said, breaking the tension. "Except for you, Lynn. Come on into the office and we'll take care of getting those tickets. They can be messengered out in the morning."

Blade watched her go without looking back at him. This plan of hers wasn't good and now she was shutting him out. He couldn't let that happen. The only way he could protect her was if he was with her and she was open with him.

He worried about it all night, and later, when he got the return call from Leroy, his worry intensified.

No one could swear to Johnny Rincon's where-abouts that morning.

THOUGH THE STREET WAS deserted when they left the club after hours, Blade kept his gaze moving, as if looking for any sign of danger, as if he expected her abductor to jump out of a doorway. His heightened awareness sent a shiver through Lynn. Not that she expected any trouble here. At least not yet…though tomorrow night might be a different story. She was certain that Blade was simply being extra cautious after what had happened to her that morning.

Still, she was unexpectedly spooked as they walked down a mostly deserted Milwaukee Avenue and found herself checking out every doorway, every parked car. The wind suddenly kicked up and a paper flew at her, making her start. The rumble of the rapid transit train on the nearby elevated tracks competed with the beat of her heart.

Blade didn't comment, but obviously sensing her emotions, he placed a hand in the middle of her back. Oddly enough, that light touch made her feel better.

"How are the feet?" he asked, as if trying to keep her mind off what was really bothering her.

"Better, Mr. Folk Medicine," she said, sounding less frazzled than she was feeling. "They hurt, but at least I'm not limping tonight."

"It's never too late to wear something more sensible."

"Or nothing at all," she murmured, unsure of

whether she meant shoes or something more provocative.

Lynn guessed Blade was wondering the same, because she sensed him go taut at the suggestion. Which in turn sparked something inside her that made her less tired and more inclined to move closer to him, and not for the sole purpose of feeling safe.

A feeling of want, of need, multiplied in her as it seemed to do at odd moments with him.

How could one man affect her so strongly?

They reached the Jeep all too soon. Blade helped her inside, his hand on her elbow jump-starting her pulse.

And after he slid into the driver's seat and started the engine, he said, "I'm surprised you had the energy to work at all after what happened this morning."

"I'm not going to stop living," Lynn protested. "Well, in a way, I suppose I have. I've stopped living *my* life. Which isn't all bad," she admitted. "I get to see how someone else lives." What she meant was she got to be near *him*. "I just wish it could be more—I don't know—fun. Spontaneous."

"That can be arranged."

"Right."

"Really." Blade made a U-turn and headed east.

"What? Where are we going?"

"Someplace where we can be spontaneous."

"You're not the type."

"What type am I?"

"Serious. Quiet. Focused."

"Boring?"

"I didn't say that."

"Maybe I read your mind."

"Then you read wrong. Besides, Cass is the mind reader, right?"

"So she says."

"Do you believe her?"

"I believe certain people have gifts that other people don't understand."

So why couldn't Cass just read her mind and tell her the details of what had happened when she'd been abducted? Lynn wondered. That would simplify everything. Why the need for hypnosis?

Then again, she'd been the one to bring it up in the first place. Cass merely had been reminding her of that with the comment about jogging her memory.

So why didn't she? What was she waiting for?

Definitely a control issue...the way she'd learned to live her life, Lynn supposed. Control issues didn't end with personal relationships. But she was certain she could trust Cass even as she trusted Blade.

So if nothing else worked...

But her heart beat a little faster just thinking about it.

Suddenly she looked up and realized they were about as far east as they could get. Lake Shore Drive loomed ahead of them. Even in the middle of the night, cars zoomed along in either direction.

"We're taking a joyride?"

"Not exactly."

As they shot under the drive, she realized only one option remained. "The beach?"

"Why not?" he asked, driving straight into the parking lot, since the gates were up.

A stroll along the beach conjured all kinds of romantic thoughts. Better thoughts than she'd had all day. She and Blade alone under a full moon...

North Avenue Beach was a testament to the good life. At a local health club's outdoor venue right next to the lake, patrons could work out on equipment or use free weights, while breathing in fresh air and a fabulous view of the downtown Chicago skyline. The new public building provided the usual changing rooms and rest rooms, but in an unusual edifice in the shape of an ocean liner. Lynn had whiled away more than one afternoon or evening eating and drinking at the rooftop restaurant.

All now, of course, deserted. Chicago parks and beaches had officially closed hours before.

Even so, they left the vehicle, took off their shoes and walked down to the water's edge. The tide rolled in over their bare feet, making Lynn jump away from the cold foam.

"The water will make you feel better," Blade promised.

"I suppose I'll have to believe you."

"Suppose?"

"Well, you were right about the tea and the salve, Mr. Folk Medicine. But what exactly is the sand and water supposed to do for me?"

"Center you. Make you one with nature."

She laughed. "I'm not a nature girl. I've never been camping in my life. Give me a fine hotel and a comfortable bed any day."

"You don't have to camp to be one with nature," Blade argued. "Have you ever stood in awe of a beautiful sunrise?"

"A few times," she admitted.

"Appreciated a beautiful landscape?"

"Of course."

"Stopped and let a breeze play over you on a hot summer day?"

"Many times."

"Then you have your own appreciation for nature. I'm just suggesting you dig a little deeper."

He held out his hand.

How could she resist?

As they continued walking north, she dug her toes into the wet sand and let her troubles go for the moment. "I've never known anyone like you before."

"Is that good or bad?"

"Yes."

"I'm half-bad?" Blade asked, his low tone sending her pulse thrumming.

"Only in the best way," Lynn insisted. "You make me feel things I never wanted to feel."

He stopped and so did she.

"Tell me," he whispered softly, turning her toward him.

The moon silvered his features, making him seem more handsome than ever. Her gaze strayed from his inky eyes down his full-bridged nose to his sculpted lips...and remained there.

"Dependent," she admitted.

"I'm sorry."

"I'm not." She met his gaze once more. "I didn't mean it that way. It's hard to explain. It's not the way my mom is with my dad. Not the way my sister Dani was with her ex-husband, Nathan, either. It's a good kind of dependence. Like I can trust you and you won't let me down. Like we have a bond that makes us..."

"What?"

"I don't know," she admitted.

She wanted to know, wanted to be able to express what she was feeling. Wanted to be able to tell Blade how very important he'd become to her in so short a time.

How she cared for him…maybe even loved him.

Dear God, did she? Could it be?

Love?

Her heartbeat thundered in her ears from a new kind of fear.

And as if he could hear, could understand exactly how confused and anxious and astounded she felt, he dipped his head and brushed his lips against hers.

She swayed toward him and locked her lips onto his and clutched at his shoulders, fearing that if she let go, she might fall.

Or he might pull away.

He wrapped his arms around her and instantly she felt better. Secure. More complete.

He would never let her fall, she thought, would never let her go.

Would never disappoint her.

He deepened the kiss and she let her head fall back so that he was bending over her, almost surrounding her. And everywhere he touched her, she burned for him. Burned for more. He was like a fever in her blood. She couldn't get enough of him, though she tried.

Her flesh quivered where he touched her, chest against her breasts, hands splayed against her back. And her middle—oh, how her middle heated from the inside out, like the core of a flame….

The lake rolled in and splashed them with icy fingers, and heat turned to steam and they jumped apart.

"I told you the water would make you feel better," Blade said, laughing.

Lynn laughed with him. "Not the water. *You*." She'd never met a man who was so nurturing before. "You make me feel so safe."

Blade groaned and held her tighter. "I want you to be safe. I don't want anything bad to happen to you. You believe that, don't you?"

He sounded desperate to convince her. And she was desperate to believe him.

"Yes," she murmured. "Yes."

"That's why…" he lightly rubbed his lips against hers, "…I don't want you messing with Johnny Rincon."

"I have to—"

"No, you don't. If Churchill and Cooper don't pan out, we'll find another way to figure out if Johnny was responsible without involving you directly. I promise I won't let him get away with it if he was the one. Trust me."

"I do trust you."

"Then don't open yourself up to him. Whether or not he's your stalker, he's too dangerous."

She sensed Blade's urgency. And she trusted him to make things right for her. "All right," she finally agreed, "I won't send the tickets to him."

Blade kissed her, long and deep, as if in reward.

At least that's the way she saw it after he too-abruptly ended the kiss and her head began to clear as they made their way back to the Jeep.

A reward for *her* doing what *he'd* wanted.

A frisson of unease crawled down Lynn's spine as she realized she'd just allowed herself to be manipulated by a man.

Chapter Twelve

Lynn knew that, but for the realization, she might have slept with Blade the night before. Instead, she'd kept to her own quarters and her own bed for the first time since moving in with him.

Unfortunately, she'd slept in fits and starts and had wakened before dawn with her emotions as fragmented as her memories.

The cold light of day brought with it a dose of good sense, however. Sleeping with Blade under any circumstances would be a big mistake. They were nothing alike, had nothing in common.

Once this was all over...

She ignored the haunting despair the thought conjured as she entered the shop to courier the concert tickets to Churchill and Cooper. The package addressed to Johnny Rincon taunted her, and part of her wanted to defy Blade for the way he had tricked her. But of course he was right. He always was. She would throw them away.

Her transaction was interrupted several times by phone calls, but at last the thing was done. She returned to the Jeep, where Blade sat, parked by the curb.

A realistic woman, she didn't live in fantasies. Opposites might attract, but two people this opposite made a romance novel, not a real-life relationship.

She tried to remember that as they arrived at his gym and began sparring, as each movement brought them into contact so deliciously painful that she suddenly called a halt to her lesson in self-defense.

"I can't do this," she told him.

"Are you hurt?"

She noted the concern in Blade's voice and the worried way he was looking at her. "No, I'm fine. Just…distracted."

"You need to focus your energies—"

"Yes, I know!"

"Then what's wrong? Are you worried about tonight? It's not too late to call it off."

"It's not tonight, not exactly." Lynn set her jaw so that she wouldn't say more, then wondered why she should hold back her resentment. "You really want to know what's wrong? It's *you!*" She lowered her voice lest anyone else in the gym hear. "I don't like being manipulated."

"I don't get it."

Irritated by his apparent confusion, she said, "I'm referring to the way you got me to agree not to invite Johnny Rincon."

"I simply appealed to your good sense."

"You appealed to a lot more than that." Like her heart. "You seduced me into agreeing."

His lips curved into a slow grin. "Trust me, Lynn, if I had seduced you, I would definitely remember that."

Not amused, she shoved past him, heading for the locker room, muttering, "This is no joke."

"Lynn, wait."

She kept going, but he caught up to her in the hallway.

"Wait," he repeated.

She whirled around to face him. "Why? So you can tell me I'm wrong?"

"So I can apologize. I didn't think of what happened between us that way. It was in the moment—a very wonderful moment, by the way—and I was desperate to convince you to stay away from Johnny. I was dead serious about wanting to keep you safe."

"You can't live my life for me."

"I'm not trying to. You must see that your world view of man-woman relationships is a little skewed—not without reason, I admit. But you're also dealing with *me,* Lynn, with someone who cares about you—"

"My father always said he cared about my mother, and Nathan said he cared about Dani."

"And I'm neither of those men. I care about you *because* you're strong and confident—well, most of the time. And because you care about others. You fight the good fight, because it's the right thing to do. I've always been very big on doing the right thing," he told her.

"I'm an adult. I can make my own decisions."

"I don't want to control you, but relationships and the ways people deal with one another get complicated sometimes. If you believe anything, then believe I simply want to make sure nothing more happens to you. And that the control thing is *your* issue, not mine."

Practically the same thing Nathan had said to her. Lynn put a hand to her face and took a deep breath.

Had history made her misjudge him the night before? Very possibly. He certainly seemed sincere now. She made an instant decision to let it go, to stop viewing Blade's every move with suspicion.

Or at least she would try.

"You're right," she admitted, looking him square in the eye. "And I'm the one who should be sorry."

"Truce?"

"Truce."

His smile was slow and sweet, and Lynn felt a hard thunk in the region of her chest.

"Then let's get back in the gym," Blade said, "and let me teach you some new moves."

NEW MOVES in her growing repertoire or not, Lynn couldn't deny the case of nerves that cursed her as she readied herself prior to Club Undercover's opening that night.

The big night. This was it. This was the moment to face the man who'd held her prisoner, and help put him behind bars. She shivered in anticipation...and dread.

Maria Savage wouldn't arrive for another hour, but her entourage had already taken over the employee lounge. The kitchen and wait staffs were scurrying around in a tizzy. And from what Lynn had been told, customers were already four deep up the stairs and along the sidewalk halfway to the corner.

She couldn't wear her usual outfit, since the waitresses in the VIP section wore simply cut sequined dresses. Rummaging through the closet, she found a deep blue number that fit her like a second skin... which presented a slight problem in that she was to be wired for sound.

To that end, she entered Gideon's office, where Cass and Logan awaited her. The mike, wire and transmitter were already laid out on the desk. She knew Logan would set up a recording device in the office behind the upstairs bar.

"Tuck the wire under a breast and run it down your side," the security chief said dispassionately. "It'll be less noticeable that way. We'll attach the transmitter to your thigh with an adjustable strap."

When he showed it to her, it reminded Lynn of the knife holster Blade wore strapped to his calf.

"Kind of like a garter," she mumbled.

No one laughed. Everyone was tense tonight.

Picking up the wire, Cass offered, "I'll help you," and Logan thoughtfully turned his back on them.

Lynn didn't see how this hot little number she was wearing was going to hide the bulge of a transmitter, not even a small, flat one. But she did as he ordered, wiggling the wire down her side until Cass could reach up and catch the end and connect it to the small black box. After which Cass taped the wire in several strategic places on her body so that it wouldn't shift and betray her.

Then came the transmitter. The best place to hide it would be between her thighs, of course, but the bulge would drive anyone who needed to walk nuts. And she'd be doing a lot of that tonight while serving drinks and food. Once her "garter" was in place, Lynn adjusted the box forward slightly—a tolerable enough position so her other thigh wouldn't be chafed and her panty hose wouldn't run.

When they finished, both wire and box seemed to be neatly out of sight, as was the tiny mike clinging inside her low-cut bodice.

By this time, Gideon and Blade had joined them, along with a man she didn't know.

"This is Gabe Conner," Gideon said. "I'm bringing him on board tonight."

"Glad to be of service," Gabe said.

Wondering how much Gideon had told the dark-haired, green-eyed stranger, Lynn merely nodded. If Gideon thought he was all right, then he was.

"Will I do?" she asked, turning slowly.

There was no mirror in the room, so Lynn had to rely on them. She looked for their approval, and the spark in Blade's gaze caught her so off guard she nearly stumbled over her own feet.

Gideon diffused the moment. "Good job. No one will be the wiser."

She blinked. "Great."

Logan opened a file folder. "I picked up photos of both Churchill and Cooper from the Internet. Keep an eye out for these two."

He passed out prints of both.

Just looking at them, Lynn had to admit Churchill appeared nearly as unpleasant as he'd been the morning before, but certainly not dangerous. Decked out in his chef's outfit, Cooper underwhelmed her. Or maybe she was making the mistake of believing that a man who cooked wouldn't be violent. She had to keep in mind he used sharp knives and other dangerous tools for a living.

Still, she had a hard time believing that either of these men were responsible for her pain.

Gideon went over the plan. "I'll stay in the VIP area all night to keep an eye on everything up there. Logan will be with me, but if one of the suspects gets up and leaves his table, Logan will follow to see what he's up to. Gabe will work the bar and act as backup. Blade, you'll oversee the downstairs, and Cass, once you've introduced Maria, you'll be Blade's eyes tonight.''

Lynn knew Blade wasn't happy—he'd been hoping to work the upstairs bar and therefore be able to watch over her himself—but he didn't protest. They would all be wired for sound with intercom headsets.

"So, ladies and gents, are we ready to rock and roll?" Gideon asked.

"Ready," came a chorus of agreement.

"Twenty minutes until show time," Cass said.

Twenty minutes to kill before the club doors opened and she had to put herself out there, a willing target for whomever had abducted her exactly one week before, Lynn realized.

She and Cass made a stop at the ladies' lounge. Lynn checked herself over in the mirror. Tonight she was a study in deep blue—hair, lips, nails and tinted glasses, plus the dress.

Was the disguise enough to protect her?

As if Cass could read her mind, she said, "He won't recognize you."

Not that it took psychic ability for anyone to figure out how spooked she was, Lynn thought.

"I'll be fine," she said, more to herself than the other woman. "I'll be fine."

"How's the memory?"

"Still fractured."

"Have you given hypnosis any more thought?"

She'd given it lots of thought, but had come to no decision. "Maybe as a last resort."

"You can trust me."

"I do." Lynn gave her a quick hug. "Thanks."

"Just breathe, okay?" Cass gave her shoulders a reassuring squeeze. "It'll be all right."

"One of your visions?"

The redhead grinned and shook her head. "It's just that we're all behind you."

A fact that Lynn appreciated.

Ten minutes to go. Unable to stand the wait, she thought she needed to keep busy, to keep her mind occupied. But everything was set up. All she had to do was walk into the VIP lounge and start working.

Not having checked her messages earlier, she decided to do so now. Thankfully, no new crisis had come up at the law firm. No doubt the partners were worried about her billing hours, because one of the paralegals had left a message saying that everyone wanted to know when she planned on returning.

"I wish I knew, folks, I wish I knew."

Then she called home. She had a single message, recorded earlier that day. Her grip tightened on the receiver as the familiar voice hissed at her.

"You think you're so clever, Evelyn, hiding out who knows where."

The urgent whisper got to her, made her stomach knot and the fine hairs at the back of her neck stand at attention.

"I've made it my business to find out…to find you. That's all I've been thinking about."

"Then do it, let's get it over with." Only this time, she would be prepared.

"You've become my obsession, Evelyn. You'll never be free of me. Not while you're alive." He laughed. *"Until we meet again…"*

The message ended with another evil laugh, and

when Lynn remembered to breathe, it came out in a gasp.

Her first thought was to tell Blade, but by the time she walked out of the office and into the downstairs foyer, it held a crush of customers waiting to gain entrance into the club. She couldn't get near the cave-like entryway or the hostess, Mags, and Lynn couldn't catch the eye of either of the bouncers who were keeping people in line.

She tried fighting the throng and for her trouble got an elbow in her side and an angry patron yelling, "Hey, wait your turn!"

Giving up, she took the stairs to get over to the special VIP street-level entrance. The sun might be down, but it was summer and therefore still light, so she kept her face averted from the VIP crowd, which was modest compared to the hordes heading downstairs. No sense in taking any chances.

At six-five, his head shaved, his coffee-colored skin glowing in the humidity, the bouncer named Par-Tee was a force to be reckoned with. No one who didn't belong in VIP seating got past him.

"Melinda, you gotta problem, baby?" Par-Tee asked.

Starting at the use of her still unfamiliar fake name, Lynn said, "I waited too long, then couldn't get through the crowd downstairs."

He unhooked the rope and let her into his space, then opened the street-level door for her.

"Hey, if you're going to let the tootsie in, then open the doors to everyone!"

Responding to the familiar voice, Lynn couldn't help herself. Her pulse jumped when she glanced back and got a glimpse of Victor Churchill, a very young, very thin and striking brunette on his arm.

Lynn slipped inside and hurried to her station, where she checked herself in on the computer she'd use to place her customers' orders.

And then she prayed that Victor Churchill hadn't gotten a good look at her face.

TONIGHT WOULD BE the night.

He had to give her credit—she might have fooled him if he hadn't already seen her days ago when she'd gone back to her office. But he had her now. His excitement had escalated as he'd watched her scurry into the building like some scared rat.

He laughed to himself. How appropriate an analogy. A rat. Vermin. That's what she was.

Now if only he had some poison…

No, that would be too easy. Then the game would be over too quickly. She would be free of pain, and he wanted her to suffer even as she'd made him suffer.

He knew, though, the only way he could do that was if she cared enough to feel gut-shot with loss if something she cared about was taken from her.

But he doubted that she cared about anything or anyone more than her high-handed opinions.

She was a cold bitch.

Maybe he would see if he could warm her up before he killed her.

STILL WORRYING that Churchill might have seen her, Lynn crossed to his table with a sense of trepidation she couldn't deny. He had the brunette and the two other couples he'd brought focused on him—older men, probably business associates, and younger, more attractive women, probably trophy dates the men's wives didn't know about.

For a moment, Lynn watched Churchill work the small crowd. He was telling a long-winded story, and his companions were into it. Deciding the businessman was already focused elsewhere and would hardly notice her, she made her approach.

"May I take your drink order?" she asked in a light, cheery voice unlike her own.

"Your best champagne all around." Churchill made a magnanimous gesture, as if he were paying for everything out of his own pocket.

"And have you had time to look at the menu?"

"I can't eat anything," the brunette said petulantly. "I have an important shoot next week. The camera puts ten pounds on a person, you know."

A model. Lynn thought the young woman could use ten pounds for real, but didn't comment. Her purpose was to get Churchill to talk.

Leaning in closer, figuring if she gave him a little cleavage he would speak right into the mike, she asked, "Appetizers?"

"I'll take *you,* honey," he said, looking straight into her eyes.

Lynn felt the blood drain from her face. He wasn't supposed to do that. Wasn't supposed to look directly at her as if he were studying her features. But if he recognized her, he wasn't registering the fact.

Hardly able to speak, she asked, "How about bruschetta?"

"How about something more tender?"

Now he was staring at her breasts.

"We have a shrimp appetizer with goat cheese," she said sweetly. *You old goat!*

"I guess that'll have to do."

He laughed heartily and looked around at his compatriots. The women were smiling tightly, while the men seemed to be trying to keep their own thoughts from showing.

And before she could get away, Lynn felt Churchill's hand on her butt. He gave her firm flesh a quick squeeze.

"Give me good service, honey, and I'll give you what you need."

The only reason Lynn didn't grab his hand and break it the way Blade had demonstrated was because then the game would be over. She wished she knew if the bastard was guilty or just an ignorant boor. Maybe he was both.

So in the interest of the night's plan, she forced a stupid grin to her lips, backed off without telling him what she thought, and escaped to her station. As she was angrily punching the order in, Gideon came up behind her.

"You have something against computers?"

"Against Churchill. Got him!" she said triumphantly, hitting the shrimp appetizer selection. "Now someone else can have him."

Though she knew that really wasn't an option at the moment, since she'd replaced one of the other waitresses for the evening.

"Cooper's a no-show, huh?" Gideon commented.

She glanced toward the vacant table. "I guess a concert and free drink and food isn't enough to lure a chef away from his Friday night specials."

"I don't know about that. I called the restaurant. Guess who took off sick tonight?"

Her eyes widened. "Then Cooper will be here."

Though when? she wondered. The concert would start soon. The place was packed…all but for that single empty table now mocking her.

BLADE KEPT HIMSELF BUSY mixing drinks and worrying. Lynn would be all right up there, he told himself. With Gideon and Logan on scene, no one would get to her.

Drink orders slowed down during the first act of the performance. The very talented Maria Savage held the audience in thrall, giving him the opportunity to take more than a cursory look around for the first time that evening.

His gaze went straight up the several levels of seating to the VIP area, which was akin to box seats, where everyone had a front-row view almost directly over the stage. He hadn't seen Lynn for a while now. Blade couldn't help but wonder if she'd gotten to Churchill and Cooper yet.

Oddly enough, one table sat empty….

He let his gaze drift farther, and then froze when he saw the man wearing sunglasses at the farthest table.

What the hell!

Blade checked his intercom—only Team Undercover and Lynn were supposed to be on channel 3.

"Mayday," he said softly. "Lynn, come in." When she didn't, he cursed softly and left the bar to his assistant. "Lynn!"

"What's wrong?" Gideon asked.

"Over at the far north end." As he headed for the stairs, Blade's gaze pinned the man sitting there.

"Who is he?"

"Johnny Rincon."

Chapter Thirteen

Lynn didn't have a clue that Blade had come up to the VIP area until he was breathing down her neck.

"Why aren't you wearing your headset?" he demanded in a low tone right next to her ear.

She gaped at his scowling face and touched her head as if expecting to feel it there. "I guess I forgot."

"Like you forgot to tell me you'd messengered the tickets to Johnny?"

"What? No!"

"Then why is he here?"

"Where?" she gasped.

Blade indicated the table in the corner.

Lynn looked past him at the man wearing sunglasses who sat alone. Not knowing how she could have missed him—maybe her aggravation with Churchill had kept her stewing blindly—she realized how dangerous one moment's inattention on her part could be.

"I never even noticed him." She met Blade's gaze and raised her voice to be certain he heard her above the music. "And I didn't send those tickets. I trashed the envelope addressed to him." Frowning, she re-

membered being angry and distracted, but couldn't
visualize the act of dropping the envelope in the can.
"Well...that's what I meant to do, anyway. Maybe I
left it on the counter and it got messengered out by
mistake."

Blade scowled harder. "Just stay away from
Johnny."

"He's not in my section," she said through
clenched teeth. Why did Blade have to put her back
up over the situation? Her voice rose another notch
as she asked, "What are you doing up here, anyway?"

"Other than keeping my eyes on you? I'll be bartending."

"Then maybe you'd better get to work."

"Shh!" A nearby customer hushed them and gave
them a poisonous look.

And as Blade stalked to the bar, she glanced over
at the far end, where Johnny sat. She couldn't tell for
sure—not with him wearing sunglasses in the darkened room—but she imagined he was staring at her.

He was simply curious, she told herself in an attempt to steady her pulse.

He couldn't possibly recognize her.

THE MOMENT MARIA SAVAGE left the stage to take
her break, the orders started flowing in, and Blade
would have been busier than he liked if Gabe Conner
hadn't been there to lend a hand. So who was Gabe,
really? Blade wondered. Gideon had been purposely
vague in making Gabe's introductions.

But at least Gabe's being there allowed him to keep
one eye on Johnny, the other on Lynn. He only hoped

she followed his orders and stayed away from the dangerous man.

His orders. She didn't want to take them. On the one hand, he couldn't blame her. On the other, he wanted to shout that this was her life, for God's sake, and was she so crazy that she would risk it over the issue of independence?

"I hear some people have been asking about me."

Setting his jaw, Blade turned to face his old enemy. "Johnny, I'm surprised to find you here. I thought Skipper's was more your speed."

"Skipper's don't have Maria Savage. Maybe you can made an introduction...for old time's sake."

"Talk to someone in her entourage. Her body-guard."

"Yeah, she needs someone to guard that body. It's almost as fine as the one on the chickie you were sweet-talking a while back. You remember her—the waitress in blue sequins."

"You mean Melinda," Blade said, being sure to use the fake name.

Johnny shrugged and Blade wanted in the worst way to know what he was thinking. Maybe that's why he wore the sunglasses even at night, even inside—so no one could read him.

"You could introduce me to this Melinda."

"Don't think so."

"Why? Does she have a bodyguard, too? *You*, maybe? Now that makes her even more interesting."

Johnny laughed, and Blade wanted to deck him, to hang him up to dry, and if he were the one who'd been stalking Lynn, to cut him again. He told himself he was more civilized than that, but part of him disagreed.

"So, back to my observation," Johnny said.

"Which one?"

"About the big interest in my whereabouts this week. You wouldn't happen to know anything about that?"

Blade spotted Lynn approaching the bar. "Why would I?"

What the hell was wrong with her? Why couldn't she cooperate?

"All this interest started right after your visit to Skipper's, Blade, buddy. Coincidence?"

"Some people believe there's no such thing," Lynn said, stopping at the bar right next to Johnny. "If you ask me, coincidences happen all the time. I need a couple of Pellegrinos, with ice," she told Blade as she directly faced his prime suspect.

Gabe was busy filling another order. Trying not to glower at her lest Johnny pick up on it, Blade grabbed a couple of glasses and filled them with ice.

"So you're Melinda."

"Either you're a mind reader or someone is telling tales out of school."

The way she was leaning into the bastard made Blade nervous. He knew she was flirting to get him to talk, trying to get close to make sure his voice got picked up.

Johnny laughed. "School. That's a good one. I never finished school, honey, but I can keep a girl like you satisfied. How about you and me—"

"No." Blade thunked down the two glasses and bottles of designer water in front of Lynn. "You'd better see to your customers."

Her satisfaction was reflected in her smile. "Now that I got what I need, I will."

"Not so fast, honey."

When Johnny put a hand on Lynn to stop her from moving off, Blade saw red. "Let go of her."

"She yours?"

"I'm no one's!" Lynn protested, which made Blade even angrier.

"Why don't you and me talk about changing that?" Johnny suggested.

When he slipped an arm around her shoulders, Blade lost it. Without thinking, he launched himself over the bar and onto the other man.

A woman screamed as they went flying, bouncing off a booth and onto the floor. As they rolled, Blade felt Johnny reaching around behind himself, as if going for his gun. Blade flashed a hand down his leg and a second later pulled it back up, holding the knife.

Slamming Johnny onto his back, his gun hand trapped under him, Blade pressed the knife tip to Johnny's good cheek.

"You made a mistake coming here and causing trouble," Blade growled.

"All right, so I made a mistake. Let me up and I'll get out."

"Should I call the cops?" Gabe asked, phone in his hand.

"No police!" Johnny yelled.

Blade realized they were surrounded by employees. Though he was tempted to nick the bastard as a warning, instead of drawing blood he withdrew the knife and stood. Lynn stepped next to him and put a hand on his arm.

"Hold that call," Blade told Gabe. "The scum is leaving."

Gideon then told Par-Tee, "Get him out of here."

"Watch him," Blade warned, "he's armed."

The bouncer grabbed Johnny and had him on his feet in seconds, his other hand snaking under the loose suit jacket and relieving him of an impressive-looking handgun, which he turned over to Logan. "Let's you and me ambulate."

"Fine."

But as they started off, Par-Tee's meaty hand surrounding his upper arm, Johnny glanced back, sunglasses still in place. His head turned from Blade to Lynn, then back to Blade, and then he mouthed, *You'll be sorry.*

"THE TWO OF YOU should take a break," Gideon suggested, indicating the door behind the bar, which led to the small office where the recorder was set up. "Gabe can take over the bar and I'll handle things here."

The customers needed handling, Lynn realized. They were abuzz with the incident, and she burned with embarrassment under their curious stares.

She barely waited until they got inside and Blade closed the door before whirling on him. "I could have handled Johnny Rincon without the violence!"

Crossing his arms over his chest, he retorted, "You don't know that."

"We had dozens of witnesses, for heaven's sake. Given the circumstances, what's the worst he could have done?"

"He was touching you!"

How possessive of Blade. Good thing he hadn't seen Churchill grabbing her butt, which had been a whole lot more personal, Lynn thought. He might have wrung the man's neck right on the spot.

"And that was worth a major incident?" she demanded hotly. "For that you had to pull a knife?"

"He was going for his gun."

Which was the reason she was so angry with Blade—because he'd put himself in danger. Because he could have been killed. "Because you attacked him!"

"I was trying to protect you."

"Reacting like you did under the circumstances went beyond protection, Blade."

"Maybe it did."

She figured that was about as close as she was going to get to an admission of any kind from him…but to what, exactly, was he admitting?

"I told you to stay away from Johnny in the first place," he reminded her.

She heard his anger, just as sharp as hers, if more under control. "No way was I going to pass up the opportunity to get his voice on tape. I'm sick of this subterfuge. I want my life back!"

He couldn't hide his knee-jerk reaction, as if she'd slapped him in the face. But before she could soften the blow, he asked, "You want your life back so much that you chanced losing it?"

"Oh, for heaven's sake, I was surrounded by testosterone—Gideon, Logan, you. And Johnny didn't recognize me. He was simply trying to provoke you by using me, because *you* made him think there was something going on between us."

"Isn't there?"

Blood rushed up her neck and into her face. She had to admit there definitely was something going on for her, whether or not it was sensible, whether or not they fit into each other's lives.

And who said they had to, anyway?

"Every time you make me think you feel something for me," she said, "you pull back."

"A bodyguard getting involved with his subject would put her at more risk."

Moving closer, she stared up into his face, which he'd schooled into a neutral expression. "Is that the real reason, Blade? Is it?"

Her anger had quickly cooled. The way he'd responded to Johnny had been personal—not because of his own history but because of her. Because he *did* care about her.

Could it be more than caring? Could he be as confused about what he was feeling as she was?

"We should get back to work," Blade said, though he didn't make a move to open the door.

"Why? Are you afraid to talk about it?" Lynn didn't care if this wasn't an appropriate time for personal business, she wanted answers. She wanted something that explained why she opened herself to a man she barely knew. Why she wanted more. "You say you care about me. How much?"

"More than makes me comfortable."

Moving so close there was barely breathing room between them, she murmured, "Maybe we're not supposed to get too comfortable with each other...."

With a groan, Blade snaked an arm behind her back and pulled her up against him. Lynn gasped, but before she could take another breath, his mouth crushed hers in a torrid kiss.

Hazily, she let herself go, let herself be engulfed in something that had no explanation, after all. What she felt for Blade was as old as time itself. She was a woman and he was a man and she wanted him. It was that simple. That natural. That crazy.

Melting against him, Lynn imagined them taking it to the next level. She was ready, so, so ready... especially when he let one hand travel downward, the other around to a breast. Her body instantly quickened as his fingers traversed the sequined material, and the exposed flesh of her breasts quivered in anticipation. Then his fingers touched her and sensation shot through her...

Until once more he pulled away from her.

Disappointed, Lynn took a shaky breath and scraped the hair back from her face, then saw that his fingers had gotten tangled in the wire she was wearing. He pulled free and they stared at each other for a moment before he tucked the device out of sight again. Another frisson of need washed through her.

Then Lynn said, "I guess we forgot ourselves for a moment." Not particularly wanting everyone to be aware of what had gone on in here, she indicated the recorder. "Know how to work that thing?"

Of a like mind, Blade rewound the tape to where they'd entered the office, and then they went back to work. Thankfully, things had simmered down and Maria Savage was back on stage and no one but Gideon and Logan seemed to notice their return.

Even so, Lynn felt uneasy, as if she were waiting for the other shoe to drop.

Or as if someone were watching her.

Churchill?

Every chance she got, she peered at the man, but he never seemed to be paying her any mind save the few times she actually approached the table.

So why, then, did she get the feeling that someone was looking over her shoulder?

Cooper? Could the creepy cannibal be here somewhere, imagining how he would make mincemeat out of her, given the chance?

He wasn't seated with the VIPs, that was for certain. His table still remained empty, and she didn't see anyone who could be him here on the VIP floor. The rest of the club was a different story, however. It was packed and thrown pretty much in the dark during the performance, and if he was out there somewhere, watching and waiting for an opportunity to get at her, then she wouldn't know because she couldn't spot him. Too many customers, too little light.

One more glance around assured her that pointmen Blade, Gideon and Logan were spread around the VIP area in a large triangle. Being surrounded by so many strong, capable guys was comforting.

As she continued to serve food and drinks throughout the performance, Lynn felt the unease settle into something less threatening. After getting two suspects on tape, one of whom had been ousted from the club, the rest of the night seemed anticlimactic.

The concert ended to a standing ovation. Maria Savage sang three encores, and then she was gone. Looking down, Lynn saw Cass hurrying to the backstage door, undoubtedly to see that the singer and crew got off without incident.

While half the audience left immediately, the other half lingered over a last drink and conversation, drifting away in small groups during the next half hour. It was early by club standards—barely midnight.

Lynn was so busy helping with the cleanup, she didn't even notice when Victor Churchill and his cronies left the club. When she suddenly realized they were gone, her sense of relief was tremendous.

''I'm going downstairs to check on the bar,'' Blade said, once the VIP lounge was clear of customers. ''And then I'll be ready to go.''

''I need to get out of this wire.''

Lynn looked around for Logan, but he, like Gideon, was downstairs, making certain that security was tight, so she headed for the office behind the bar alone.

Once there, she turned off the recorder, removed the transmitter from her thigh and unfastened the mike from her bodice. Removing the sticky tape that held the wire in place on her body wasn't fun, but she gritted her teeth and did so as speedily as she could.

Now if only her efforts paid off.

Taping Johnny Rincon tonight was a bonus she hadn't counted on. Certain that she'd gotten enough of his voice so that he would either be in or out, according to the acoustical expert, she felt they'd done a good night's work.

She left the equipment and tape for Logan.

Her sense of accomplishment followed her out the door into the darkened bar area. The place was unnaturally quiet. A shiver crept down her spine, but she told herself that all was well in her world tonight, that she had no immediate need for worry.

About to head for the stairs, she heard a swish behind her...like a rest room door shutting.

''Blade?'' she called.

But even as she started to turn in that direction, something hard poked her in the back and a whispered voice in her ear made her skin crawl.

"Don't turn around, don't say a word." A click that sounded like the hammer of a revolver being pulled back was followed by his threat: "You bring anyone else into this and not only are you dead, but so is he."

Chapter Fourteen

Ready to leave, Blade wondered what was taking Lynn so long. Was she having trouble getting out of the wire?

Intending to help her, he started up the stairs, but when he was almost to the upper level, he heard a scuffle.

"Lynn?"

When she didn't answer, he sprinted the rest of the way, arriving in time to see the emergency exit door on the alley swinging shut.

"What the hell?"

Any remaining employees were downstairs. Any but Lynn. Why in the world would she go out into the alley?

Unless it hadn't been her idea...

He bolted for the door and thrust it open. A dark-garbed man wearing a ski mask was hauling Lynn toward a car. Blindfolded, her hands tied behind her, she stumbled and almost fell to her knees.

Blade flew forward, letting the emergency door slam shut behind him. The noise alerted the man, who took one look his way before shoving Lynn toward him, and in the process, dropped car keys that flew along the ground. Lynn fell to her knees and the villain immediately beat a fast retreat down the alley on foot.

"Lynn—"

"I'm okay, I'm okay."

Even knowing the bastard would probably get away, Blade couldn't leave her there like that. He helped her to her feet, then ripped off the blindfold.

"Who?" she asked. "Rincon?"

Indeed, Johnny would be the logical choice. But Blade had to admit, "I didn't see his face," as he loosened the webbed strap that secured her wrists behind her back. "Get Gideon and Logan—I'm going after him!"

"Blade, no! What if he shoots at you?"

But blinded to any danger except that to Lynn, he was already on his way. After the man's head start, Blade's chances of catching up were slim to none. But you never knew when your enemy could slip up, make a mistake. And then everything could change in a heartbeat.

Catching a glimpse of Lynn's attacker down the alley, Blade put on some speed. He'd been taught several effective ways of killing a man with his bare hands, and part of him, the primal man who hadn't gotten turned off just because he'd resigned from the military, longed to use one of them.

He focused on the dark figure, allowed himself no distractions.

Slowly, the distance between them narrowed.

The other man threw a wild glance over his shoulder—he was still wearing the hood. He seemed to be searching for some escape route, and to Blade's surprise, he hopped onto the top of a big Dumpster and from there reached up and caught on to the metal frame of an exterior metal fire escape. The man was in fine physical shape, Blade noted, again wondering if he was dealing with Johnny. The masked man easily swung himself up and onto the landing, then scrambled to his feet and took to the stairs.

Whoever he was, the villain made it about halfway to the top before Blade reached the Dumpster and followed his route.

Part of him wanted the bastard to try something, to pull that gun again, to give him an excuse. He'd hurt Lynn, had terrorized her, and now it was time for some turnaround. It was a pity Blade was too civilized to kill anyone except in self-defense.

He'd climbed the first of four levels when the man above stopped and picked up a barbeque grill someone had left on a landing. Blade couldn't get out of the way quickly enough to avoid the ash raining down on him. Eyes and nose stinging, he held his breath and pressed himself against the building as the metal grill clanged down the fire escape and then bounced off his shoulder.

Cursing, gritty eyes and all, he took the next set of stairs. Above him, Lynn's attacker had reached the top landing and was now using a narrow ladder attached to the building to get to the roof. A few seconds after he disappeared from view, two shots rang out into the night and from somewhere below, worried voices responded.

Ignoring anything but getting to the bastard before he hurt someone else, Blade forced himself to climb faster, but by the time he got all the way up, the other man was nowhere to be seen.

The roof door…

Sure enough, those shots had shattered the lock. Blade threw open the door and faced a dark deeper and more dangerous than the night surrounding him.

Without hesitating, he plunged inside.

He stood in the dark—silently, allowing his senses to adjust. A whir and clunk told him the elevator was in operation. A faint haze of light helped him locate the stairs, but still he descended more by instinct than by sight until he got down to the third floor, where light shone from a curtained window down the hall.

This old dusty building was a lair, a maze filled with odd shops and artists' studios. Cheap rent, cheap landlord. Blade doubted much was up to code.

The elevator itself was old and slow, while he was young and quick. By the time he touched down on the second floor, he was even with the metallic groans. And he got to the ground floor and shot down the hall even as the doors started to open.

Ready to go for his knife, Blade froze when he realized the lone occupant was a woman with a pierced eyebrow, nose ring and tattoos down both arms...undoubtedly a commercial tenant, who seemed as shocked to see him at this late hour as he was to see her.

Though he immediately backed off, she scurried out of the elevator toward the street door.

Leaving him wondering where the hell in this rabbit warren the viper might be hiding.

When they all gathered in Gideon's office, Blade tightly said, "It's time for you to disappear, Lynn."

Aghast at his suggestion, she stared at him. "I already did disappear—"

"For real," Blade added. "This time leaving no

trace. And you can't come back until we nail this bastard.''

"I have to agree," Gideon said. "Your attacker figured out he could find you here—"

"But how?" Lynn asked.

"—and he penetrated your disguise."

"You're not safe here anymore," Cass agreed.

"Sometimes disappearing into thin air is the best defense," Gabe said.

"You're not safe *with me*."

The last came from Blade. He wanted to send her away, Lynn realized, her horror growing. And just when she was beginning to realize her true depth of feeling for him.

Before she could think of a convincing counter argument, Logan entered the office, followed by Stella Jacobek.

The detective wanted the whole story—every detail—from the start of the evening on.

Lynn sat silently as Blade took over, giving his friend the skinny, ending with, "We could have searched the whole building for the bastard, but it probably would have been a waste of our time. For all I know, he could have fooled me, could have still been on the roof, and once I went inside, he could have used the fire escape to get away."

Stella shook her head. "Guard Lynn—that's what you were supposed to do."

"I know I let you down—"

"You went too far!" Stella looked around the room, her gaze stopping on Gabe and narrowing for a second. "You're all in on this, aren't you? Some kind of a conspiracy. Why didn't I see this before?"

"You didn't want to see," Blade said. "You don't have to see now."

He was talking in a code that Stella understood, if her expression was any indication, Lynn thought, even as she said, "Everyone here was simply trying to protect me." And she didn't want to bring them trouble.

Stella narrowed her gaze on Blade. "I thought it was odd, your coming to me and volunteering to play bodyguard."

A statement that stunned Lynn, who'd thought all along that Stella had asked Blade for his help.

"Don't read anything into it."

But Stella obviously was. She looked from one to the other of them. "Ex-military man. Ex-cop. Ex-jailbird—"

"Hey!" Cass piped up.

"I thought that was a bit softer than ex-con." Stella then moved her narrowed gaze from Gabe to Gideon. "What about you two? Who are *you* really?"

Gabe didn't say a word.

Gideon kept his gaze steady when he said, "What you see is what you get. I own this club."

"And run this operation?"

No one answered until Lynn said, "Stella, you have to keep these speculations to yourself."

"Do I?"

"Please," Lynn pleaded. "You brought me here so that I would be safe. And I would have been if I hadn't insisted on getting the suspects on tape. So it was my own fault. And if you hadn't brought me somewhere I felt safe to start with, I would have run. Well, I'm not running now. And everyone here is on our side—yours and mine."

Her speech registered with the detective; Lynn could see it in Stella's expression.

"I wouldn't be opposed to keeping what I know about this operation to myself," Stella said, "but I'm not comfortable doing that if you're going to take these ridiculous chances with your life. And I don't only mean Lynn." She peered around the room, touching each of them with her steady gaze. "I mean all of you."

The men in the room sat silent and looking testy. Cass wore a knowing expression, but Lynn didn't know what to think. To her, it sounded like the game might be over.

"You won't tell," Cass suddenly said to Stella.

"Don't be too sure of yourself."

"I am sure. I know. You wouldn't betray us like that. You only wish you'd had people like us to turn to when *you* needed help."

All ears in the room seemed to perk up at that statement, and Lynn swore that the good detective blanched. Cass had hit a nerve. A lucky guess?

Or was her ability to know things about people real?

"What's that?" Blade asked. "Stella…?"

"All right! I won't say anything to anyone," she hastily agreed. "At least not yet."

"Not ever," Cass said, her voice practically mesmerizing. "Because you wouldn't want to punish any of us for helping others who have nowhere else to turn. Not when you know what that's like."

The room seemed to hold its breath, as did the detective herself. Lynn knew that somehow this was a defining moment for the survival of Team Undercover.

Finally, Stella gave them a sharp nod of agreement. "Just promise me you'll leave it alone from here on in. Leave the detective work to me."

No one said a word.

Stella lifted her chin. "Great, it's all settled then."

Perhaps for the detective, who was obviously feeling cornered and wanting to be off the hook and so reading into their silence what made her most comfortable, Lynn thought. But nothing was settled for her. They might all want her out of harm's way, but she wasn't planning on going anywhere at the moment but home with Blade.

Thankfully, Stella took the stuffing out of them all—or perhaps banded them together more tightly—for when Lynn asked to go home, no one argued with her.

At least not until she and Blade were settled in the Jeep and heading down Milwaukee Avenue.

"Maybe tonight would be a good night for that hotel you wanted to find," he suggested.

"And maybe not."

"I'm looking out for your best interests."

"Are you sure it's not *your* best interests?" she countered, thinking this was as much about him as it was about her. Or was it about *them?*

"Don't fight me on this, Lynn."

"Don't tell me what to do!"

"It's for your own good!"

How many times, growing up had she heard those exact words? she wondered as he parked the car behind his building. Her father had constantly told her and her sisters and their mother that very same thing. It didn't matter that this could be a case of life and death for her. That Blade had real cause for his trying

to get her to listen to what he considered reason. The
sting didn't feel any less intense.

She waited until she'd climbed the stairs and was
nearly out of breath before she said, "I hate this."
Turning her back on him, she jammed her key in the
door lock.

"I know you hate it, Lynn. That's why I'm trying
to give you options."

"I'm not talking about living here or even about
my being a victim of violence." She threw open the
door and stepped inside, knowing Blade was right behind her. She spun around to face him directly. "I'm
talking about being a victim of *you.*"

How could this have happened to her? she wondered as he closed and locked the door behind him.
After swearing she would never emulate her mother,
swearing she would never get into a relationship with
a controlling man, how could she have fallen in love
with Blade Stone?

"Victim of *me?*" he asked, both his expression and
tone astounded. "I only want you to be safe."

"You want to send me away!"

That was the real problem, Lynn realized. Finally,
she was ready to admit that she was madly in love
with him. Why else would she be experiencing such
separation anxiety? But Blade couldn't decide how he
felt about her, so rather than resolve that, he was re-
jecting her by doing the very thing that would drive
her away.

Though he said, "What I want doesn't count if it
interferes with your safety."

"What is that, really?" she asked.

"To protect you."

She ignored the warning shiver the word *protect*

sent up her spine, and told herself that she was being overly sensitive to something natural and normal, if one person cared about another. More than once he'd said he cared...but how much?

"And that's it?" she asked softly. "You don't want anything else? If you do, tell me, Blade, before the opportunity passes. Before it's too late. Or am I being foolish in thinking you might want more...even as I do?"

With the groan of a man defeated by his own emotions, Blade said, "I want *you.*"

Their gazes locked and Lynn's heart hammered so hard that her chest hurt. This was it. Forget danger and safety and arguments that no one could win. This was the moment. The possibility for a future together.

"Then have me," she offered softly.

Warmth flushed through her, and for a tiny second, she didn't think he was going to take her up on her challenge. And then he stepped toward her and she practically melted against him, so closely she imagined his heart beat in sync with her own, that their two hearts were beating as one.

Then Blade was kissing her, dancing her backward toward the couch. Her thighs banged up against the arm and he kept pushing, so that she fell over it and he came down with her. But as he had done before, he threw out a hand and braced his weight on it so that he didn't crush her.

So that he didn't hurt her, she thought.

Blade would never do anything to hurt her.

His protecting her started to sound good.

He dipped his head and nuzzled her breasts. Liquid heat spread through her as fast as a wildfire.

But with Blade, she was safe, Lynn thought hazily.

Real fires wouldn't get her. A crazed stalker wouldn't get her. Only *he* would get her, and she wanted that more than anything.

He caught the lower edge of her top with his teeth and pulled it upward so slowly that she couldn't stand the wait. She reached down and tugged it up over her head, and while her hands were busy, he nipped at her through her bra, then used his tongue to lave a wet trail down her stomach. Her flesh responded and her hips rose to meet his mouth. He bit into her trousers and tried to drag them down, then gave up, backed off the couch and used his hands to remove them.

A moment later she lay there nude, legs still hooked over the arm of the couch, like a wanton.

Quickly removing his own clothes, Blade then reached down and slid her toward him, so that her hips were raised and her thighs fell open. He kissed a trail downward from her navel to her exposed center, which pooled with thick juices that he drank in.

Lynn gasped and arched as his tongue slid inside her and probed her soft depths. She spread herself wider, reaching out for him, wanting to touch him, to give him pleasure in return, but she could only finger his hair. She removed the leather wrap that secured his locks, releasing a thick curtain over his shoulders and back.

He slid up and kissed her again and again, his hair veiling their faces, his leather pouch puddling against her throat. Pulling the thong over his head and dropping the pouch to the floor, she tangled her fingers in the dark, shiny strands and gave him her heart through her lips.

When he broke the kiss and nipped her bottom lip,

she made a small pleasurable sound deep at the back of her throat that made him smile against her mouth. He then traded her mouth for her neck, neck for her breasts, breasts for her belly. Sliding both arms between her thighs, he opened her and once more feasted on her sensitive flesh.

Her pleasure grew and expanded and she needed more. She needed him.

Just as she thought she couldn't stand the spiraling sensations, he lifted his head and pulled her closer until the tip of his erection pressed against her entrance. She let him in and he pushed inside her along the smooth, wet trail he'd created for himself. When he was in fully, she cried out and arched higher, and he began a slow, torturous movement deep inside her.

"Please," she gasped as the pleasure-pressure built, "please."

In answer, he slipped his hand between them, finding her swollen and ultrasensitive. A few long, lingering strokes along her trigger set wave after wave of pleasure shuddering through her.

Then Blade stroked her himself, inside, going hard and deep and fast. Even as she shattered in reaction, he, too, cried out, and she felt him shudder within her.

This time when he fell to the couch, he didn't hold himself back. He was in her, on her, limbs tangled with hers.

"I love you," she whispered, holding him close.

At last they were one.

THE PHONE PULLED LYNN up from a deep sleep. Still tangled with Blade, although now in his bed—they'd made love everywhere along the way—she reluctantly pushed herself up and away from him, taking a moment to memorize every inch of his beautiful flesh before getting out of bed.

The phone was insistent.

Dragging a sheet to wrap around herself, she grabbed the receiver. "Hello."

"Lynn? It's Logan."

"Is something wrong?"

"I got the tape from last night to my friend in the lab first thing this morning. He's already analyzed Churchill's and Rincon's voices."

Her throat tightened. "And?"

"And they're *both* eliminated."

"What?"

"Neither one matches the speech patterns of your abductor. That leaves—"

"Timothy Cooper," she finished, remembering his result had been neutral, because she hadn't gotten him to talk enough. "Thanks, Logan. Later."

She felt Blade's breath on her hair before he asked, "What's this about Timothy Cooper?"

He nuzzled the nape of her neck, sending renewed desire shooting through her. She arched back and his hands found her breasts, thumbs lightly thrumming her nipples, creating more waves of pleasure.

"Process of elimination says he's the one," she choked out, turning in Blade's arms and moaning when she realized he was still stark naked, his long dark hair framing his face and shoulders. "Logan already had the tape from last night analyzed."

"So it *wasn't* Johnny?"

She shook her head. "Nor Churchill."

"Stella will want to know. I should call her right away," he said, though he made no move to do so.

"Tell her to take a real close look at Timothy Cooper. He's the one."

"I'll call her now. As soon as we…"

He dipped his head as if to kiss her, but she avoided him, laughing. "Make that call."

Grumbling, he did as she demanded, while she stepped into the bathroom for a fast shower. Afterward, realizing he was still on the phone with Stella, she went into her quarters, where she pulled on a comfortable pair of trousers and a top from her own wardrobe.

Then she began to gather the clothes they'd so carelessly discarded the night before. Her foot kicked something soft that scooted across the floor. His leather pouch. The impact had loosened the drawstring and its mouth had opened.

Damn!

She stooped to gather up the spilled contents—a couple of smooth stones and a yellowed newspaper clipping.

The word *Dead* caught her eye, and curious, she unfolded the clipping to see the whole headline— Dead Woman Slain—accompanied by a photograph.

Lynn felt as if her heart had stopped. The photograph was of her sister Lorraine, lying facedown in the street.

Dead…

Chapter Fifteen

Lynn was still staring at the clipping when she sensed Blade behind her.

"I just got off the phone with Stella—"

Whipping around, she waved the clipping under his nose. "I don't understand. Why do you have this?"

He blanched and swore softly, and Lynn started feeling sick inside though she didn't know why. Blade seemed to pull into himself. One minute he was hers—all sexy smiles and playful hands—the next he was a stranger.

"Why?" she demanded again, her voice a choked whisper.

He was wearing nothing but briefs, and she had to force herself to keep her gaze locked with his. For a moment, she thought perhaps the only way to get him to answer was to beat it out of him, but then he shook his head and sat on the arm of the couch where they'd made love the night before.

"We were working Black Ops as part of the new Homeland Security program," he began, "a secret mission in response to information on a terrorist train-ing camp sequestered on the northwest side of Chicago. These were dangerous men, Lynn, training to kill innocent people.''

The northwest side…where she'd sent her sister.

Lynn swallowed hard and asked, ''You went in to kill these men?''

''We went in to stop them. And yes, we were authorized to use force if necessary. This isn't murder we're talking about, it was war, right here on our own soil. These men had to be stopped. Unfortunately, someone—an informant, no doubt—leaked word of the strike and we were ambushed.'' His expression changed, filling with such pain that she could almost feel it. ''People on both sides died.''

''Including my sister Lorraine…and I was the one who sent her into the middle of that horror! Do you know who killed her, Blade? Did *he* die, too?''

''No. He's alive, Lynn.''

Her pulse jumped. ''Then you know who did it?''

''Intimately,'' he agreed. ''He's…''

She felt her pulse tick in her throat as she waited for a name.

''He's me.''

Whatever she'd expected him to tell her, she wasn't prepared for this. ''Wh-what?'' She had to have misunderstood.

''I'd just been hit myself, and then I heard someone behind me and I didn't have time to think. I fired as I turned. I thought it was a kill or be killed situation. I really didn't even see the woman until she was on the ground. Now I see her in my mind every day of my life.''

His explanation was a knife to her heart.

''You killed Lorraine?'' Her eyes stung, but Lynn

refused to let the tears flow. "And then you hid that fact like some coward?"

"I'm responsible, and given a chance, I would have owned up to it publicly. But the next thing I knew I was dragged away by one of the other men, and then I passed out. I woke up in a military hospital bed. The cover-up had already started. Those were sensitive times. No one was going to admit an operation had gone that bad. Every terrorist was either dead or taken off to a jail cell. All the evidence of what happened that night was carefully eradicated."

"Except for my sister's body," Lynn said, blinking through her watery image of him. Tears rolled down both cheeks as she remembered the funeral. "No wonder the police never got anywhere tracking down her murderer."

Blade rose and moved toward her. "Lynn..." He put out a hand, but she slapped it away.

"No! Don't touch me! The thing I really need to know...the thing that's tearing me up inside...is how the hell did I end up sleeping with my own sister's murderer?"

"Because I sought you out," he admitted. "I made it my business to know who you were. All of you. The family who survived the woman I killed. The guilt was killing *me,* Lynn, eating me alive. I was lost. I lay awake most nights trying to figure out what I could do to somehow make up for my mistake. And then I saw the news—that you'd been taken prisoner and the bastard was on the loose and still threatening you. And I saw it as my chance to make amends. If I could save you..."

Damn him! Damn his haunted expression! Damn his guilt!

"So, to make amends for my sister's murder, you slept with me?"

"I fought it, you know I did—remember that first night here? I volunteered to guard you with my life. I would give my life for yours—"

"Now there's a line if I ever heard one!" she snapped. "Sorry if I'm not impressed."

"It's true, Lynn. I *would* give up my life if it meant saving yours. At first it was to make up for your sister. But now it's so much more. I didn't intend to fall in love with you, but I did."

"Liar," she whispered, backing off from him.

"Lynn, please, you have to believe—"

"Nothing you say, Blade. I don't have to believe you, not after you made a fool of me. And I don't have to stay here, either."

He stood in painful silence and watched her open her closet, pull out her suitcase and gather an armload of clothing from the rack. She threw the garments, hangers and all, into the open case.

"Don't do this, Lynn."

"Don't do what? Go back to my real life? Or do you mean don't wake up to what you really are?"

"Don't cut me off—"

"I already have."

She looked at the mound spilling out of her suitcase and knew she would never get the damned thing closed again. And there was more stuff in her closet....

Of course there were too many things, she was trying to pack her Melinda Parker disguise. She pushed the suitcase away from her in disgust.

"I'll send someone to get my things," she said. "*My* things. *Evelyn Cross's* things."

She grabbed her purse and tried to get to the door, but he blocked her.

"Where are you going?"

"Home."

"That could be dangerous."

"*You* are dangerous." With that she ducked through the bathroom and into his quarters. When she realized he was following her, his own clothes from the night before in hand, she said, "All this time you've been lecturing me about how you wanted to protect me, how you wanted me to be safe." She opened the door to the outside. "With you, I was in more danger than I ever realized."

Escaping him, she ran.

"Lynn, wait! At least let me drive you home!"

Halfway to the stairs, she glanced back to see him trying to pull on jeans while juggling boots and a shirt, and trying to close the door behind him.

Refusing to answer, she took off as fast as she could go, scrambling between buildings toward the street, away from his Jeep. By the time he got to it and brought it around the block, she would be long gone.

But to where? She needed to catch her emotional breath.

Cass. She could go to Cass.

Lynn practically ran the half mile to the other woman's place, swiping at the tears that continued to defy her, praying all the while that her friend would be home. When she got there and laid on the bell, for a moment she thought it was too late, that Cass had gone out for the day.

Then a sleepy voice called down, "Who's there?" and Lynn could breathe again.

A few minutes later they were sharing strong coffee and heartbreak. Cass was wearing a nightshirt and bunny slippers, her hair was tangled every which way and her face was devoid of makeup. And looking at her like this, so very different from the charismatic, glamorous woman she saw every night, Lynn realized Cass had been wearing a disguise all along, too.

"Oh, honey, I'm so sorry," Cass said, hugging her tightly. "I can understand how you're devastated. But Blade—"

"No buts," Lynn whispered. "Please, no buts."

Cass nodded. "Whatever you want."

Lynn gripped her coffee mug with white-knuckled fingers. "I want this to be over, once and for all. I want an end to the torment, to not knowing not if, but when that bastard is going to come after me. Cooper, not Blade."

"Uh-huh."

"I want you to help me."

"Anything."

"Then hypnotize me." Even as she said the word, Lynn's stomach knotted and she felt her heart lurch into her throat. She'd never voluntarily given up such control before. "I need to remember everything, enough to put Cooper behind bars. Then I'll be safe."

"You're sure."

"I've never been this sure of anything."

Except for Blade, an inner voice taunted her. *And look how that turned out.*

"All right," Cass agreed. "Come this way."

Cass led her through the dining and living area into a sunroom, filled with plants that surrounded a wicker chair and a matching chaise and ottoman.

"Make yourself comfortable," Cass murmured as

she adjusted the blinds so that the area was thrown into shadow.

Then she left the room for a moment, and Lynn slipped onto the chaise longue and gripped the wicker arms hard. She tried to prepare herself for the experience. She had to do this...had to—

"Relax already."

Cass was back. She pulled the chair closer, so that she could look Lynn directly in the eye. Then she lifted what she'd left the room for—a crystal on a chain.

"Look into the facets and concentrate on the flickering light inside. Take deep, slow breaths."

"This is supposed to hypnotize me?"

"Relax. Let go of everything. Concentrate on my voice and the crystal."

She was trying. "And then what?"

"Relax your body. Feel how your toes are tingling...your feet... Let the tingle spread along your calves, your thighs, and leave behind a trail of warmth...."

Focusing on the crystal and Cass's voice, Lynn felt the tingle turn to warmth.

"Now your fingers...your forearms...deep, slow breaths...and the warmth is spreading faster now, coming together in the middle. Spreading up your neck...your face...your mind...."

The light in the crystal shifted slightly.

"Are you relaxed?"

"Uh-huh."

"Then I'm going to take you back a week to last Friday night," Cass said, her voice gentle. "But I'm going to be with you this time, so you'll be safe. You trust me, don't you?"

"Yes."

"And you feel warm and safe inside."

"Safe," Lynn whispered in agreement.

"Don't take your eyes off the crystal. We're safe inside the crystal. No one can hurt us there. Take my hand...."

Lynn clasped hands with Cass and suddenly they were leaving the lobby of her building.

"Tell me what you see."

"Darkness."

Her eyes were bound and her head felt light, and she heard that voice, that wretched taunting voice that wanted her to think she was going to die.

"You think you're so smart, bitch...have you in my power. I can do anything...not a thing you can do to stop me."

Hearing his whisper clearly in her mind, Lynn said, "He's there behind me."

Cass's voice came through a fog. "He can't hurt you. Remember that. He'll tell you who he is, Lynn, if you listen hard enough."

"After what you made me lose...play with you and let you go...could be anywhere at any time...looking over your shoulder forever..."

"Until we meet again," Lynn whispered.

"Are you still connected?" Cass asked.

"Uh-huh. Can't see him, though."

"Concentrate."

Lynn delved deeper into her mind and listened more intently.

"You've needed a man for a long time, Evelyn...shows you what it means to be accountable."

Blade...

"She was the center of my universe until you got between us."

"He hates me," she murmured. "I can feel it."

She felt him squeeze her breast.

Cooper, not Blade.

It made her feel sick inside.

"You know what that does for me? Nothing. You're not her!"

He squeezed again, harder, and she jerked once and it was gone. The voice in her head. The memories. Gone.

"Come back, you bastard."

"Lynn?"

"He's gone."

"Then I'm going to bring you back. The warmth is receding and your body is beginning to awaken. Sensation is filling you again...spreading to your limbs, fingers, toes. I'm going to remove the crystal...and you'll be awake and remember everything."

Lynn blinked and the entrancing sparkle was gone. She was looking into Cass's kind face. Cass gave her a minute, then asked her to repeat everything she remembered so the memory would now stay with her.

"That's it," Lynn said when she'd finished. "We know it's Timothy Cooper, but as far as being able to testify to that before he gets to me again..." She shook her head. "No big new revelation."

"That you recognize. Maybe you just need to think about what he said more and it'll come to you." Still holding her hand, Cass gave it an encouraging squeeze.

"I hope you're right, because I'm going back to my life, Cass. Today. No more Melinda Parker. No more Club Undercover."

"No more Blade?"

Her throat closed. "No more."

"Are you sure? You're conflicted, I know, but Blade would take a bullet for you."

"What? Did he go around telling everyone that he would gladly give up his life for mine?"

Could it be true?

"He didn't tell me anything."

"Then how did you know…?"

Staring into Cass's wide gray eyes, Lynn was suddenly spooked. The other woman had seen something about Blade and her. And Lynn knew she wouldn't explain. Cass's predictions were always cryptic, like the thing with Stella.

If Lynn believed, of course.

The thought of Blade dying for her was too horrific to contemplate, made her stomach knot and her throat close. Another person she loved dead…and because of her.

"He doesn't really die, does he?" she whispered.

"That would be up to you."

Up to her?

Lynn tried not to freak out at the thought. She didn't want to be responsible for another person's death. Especially not Blade's. How could she ever live with that knowledge? She might never want to see him again, but she certainly didn't wish him harm, didn't want him to die.

No more than Blade had wanted to be responsible for Lorraine's death, her inner voice acknowledged.

"Tell me more."

Cass shook her head. "It doesn't work that way. It's not as if I see these things like a movie with

structure. It's more like the coming attractions.
Flashes of insight to get your attention. I'm sorry.''

So a new worry plagued Lynn all the way home.
Fearing she might forget something, she went over
and over what she'd remembered under hypnosis.
Cass had told her to think about what he'd said, and
something might come to her.

*She was the center of my universe until you got
between us.*

Why did she remember that one line more than the
others?

Why couldn't she come up with the proof necessary to have Cooper arrested? Then she wouldn't have
to worry about Blade.

Even as she thought it, her inner voice called her
a liar. She would always worry, always care about
Blade. No matter what he'd done, no matter that he'd
kept the details of her sister's death from her until
she'd found the clipping, no matter that he'd made a
fool of her, she loved him.

If only he had told her the truth up front...

But if he had, would she have listened and understood his pain? Or would she have rejected him—and
his offer of help—outright?

Though distracted by what-ifs, Lynn had enough
sense to take a good look at her surroundings and
make sure she had an all-clear before getting out of
the taxi and rushing into the foyer of her high-rise.

"Ms. Cross, good to you see you," Tony said.
Then a puzzled look crossed the security guard's features. "Did you do something different...."

He indicated her hair, and Lynn smiled. "I'm ex-
perimenting," she told him. "Tony, I heard about that
break-in the night I left. I know this may sound silly,

but would you mind seeing me up to my apartment, making sure everything is okay?''

''No problem. And it's not silly.'' He came around the desk and walked with her toward the elevators. ''Say, that guy you left with the other night? He was here looking for you.''

Blade had been there? Her chest tightened. His possible presence shouldn't affect her so, not when she could no longer trust him.

''When?''

''Nearly an hour ago. When I told him you weren't here, he decided to wait. He left five, maybe ten minutes ago. The way he was pacing…well, he was making me nervous, so I was glad to see him go. I thought you oughta know.''

What if Blade had been there for other than personal reasons?

What if he'd been trying to warn her about some new danger?

Blade would take a bullet for you. Cass had told her that.

What else had Cass seen? What might have happened in her coming attractions?

He doesn't really die, does he?

That would be up to you….

Why was she dwelling on something so intangible? Why couldn't she get those thoughts out of her head? Blade was out of it now.

Even though she wasn't alone, Lynn could feel her pulse race faster as the elevator brought her closer to her floor, and she had a hard time breathing when they stood before her front door. Once inside, Tony checked every nook and cranny, every closet. He even looked under her bed. Nothing. Her apprehension was for naught.

When he was ready to leave, she said, "Thank you so much," and tried to give him a twenty.

Tony put his hands behind his back. "I wouldn't think of taking your money, Ms. Cross, not after what you went through last week. Helping you out was my pleasure."

She thanked the security guard again and double-locked the door behind him.

Being home and taking back her life didn't feel as good as she'd thought it would. She looked out at the river and Navy Pier and the park before it, but for once its beauty didn't awe her with the old intensity. A real neighborhood with big trees seemed equally appealing. As for the apartment, it suddenly seemed big and cold, and she wished for something cozier with lots of plants instead of sculptures.

Damn Blade! A few days with him had changed how she saw things. He made her want what she couldn't have—and that included a life with him.

Trying to distract herself, she checked to see if anyone had called. One message. Thinking that maybe this was Blade, when she retrieved it she was amazed to hear her sister Dani's voice instead.

"Darn, I was hoping you were going to be home. Mom told me about the attack and that you weren't staying at your place. I'm so sorry, Lynn. It must have been horrible for you. I hope you get this message, because Mom also said Nathan wheedled information out of her about my being in London. You've got to talk to her about that. She can't give him my number or address. He can't ever find me."

Lynn was caught by the way her sister's voice rose, as if in panic.

"I never told you everything that happened, Lynn. I—I'm afraid of Nathan. Don't trust anything he tells you. He…he hurt me. That's why I left him. I—I should have told you. Call me, okay?"

Nathan had hurt Dani? Why hadn't she ever said anything? Lynn wondered as she frantically dialed her sister's number. She also wondered why she'd been foolish enough to ignore her own instincts and believe Nathan.

He'd said, "She's my life, my world."

Not so far off from, "She was the center of my universe…."

The call went through to a recorded message. Lynn swore softly, then after the beep, said, "Dani, I'm home now. Call me the moment you hear this. I have to talk to you about Nathan—"

The phone went dead.

Whipping around, she saw the line dangling from a gloved hand.

"Now what was it you wanted to tell Dani about me?"

Nathan threw down the spare keys she usually kept at her computer desk, and Lynn knew exactly how dangerous he really was.

Chapter Sixteen

Not knowing where Lynn was made Blade crazy with worry. She wasn't at home. Wasn't at the law office. He didn't even know where to go next.

He never should have told her about her sister. And if he hadn't made love to her, he wouldn't have had to do any explaining. She never would have found the clipping he'd been carrying in his pouch, the constant reminder of a wrong he'd had to right.

Now Lynn had taken the opportunity out of his hands.

Now she hated him, wanted nothing to do with him, and there wasn't a damn thing he could do about it.

For the first time in his life, Blade wished he owned a cell phone. That way he could call around and ask about Lynn while driving to the next location. But what was next? He hadn't a clue, so when he saw an empty parking spot, he swung his Jeep into it and went in search of a pay phone.

First he tried Stella's cell, but got her voice mail, so he left a message that Lynn had decided to shed her disguise and now he couldn't find her.

She had to be somewhere, he thought, dreading the obvious—that Cooper had gotten hold of her again.

He called Gideon next, thinking to alert him that this operation might come back to bite him. The club owner didn't sound worried, not about himself.

"Lynn's pretty resourceful, but just in case, I'll alert Logan. He and I can help you look for her, if that's what it takes."

"Thanks. I would consider it a personal favor."

"So the do-over backfired on you?"

"Blew up in my face."

"Sorry to hear that, Blade. Everyone deserves a second chance."

Gideon's motto, Blade thought, as he dialed Cass.

Upon picking up the phone, she said, "Blade," as though she knew for sure he was on the other end. "Lynn already left, about a half hour ago."

"She was with you?" Why hadn't he thought of that? "Where did she go?"

"Home."

Blade cursed. "I must've just missed her!"

"Then get back there fast…and, Blade…be really, *really* careful."

The last sent a chill up his spine. "You saw something?"

"It's bad, Blade. He means to kill her this time. So go!"

He was gone.

Tearing out of his parking space, he drove down the street like a madman.

But when he got close to North Michigan Avenue, traffic slowed him for several minutes. Cursing, Blade was about to abandon the Jeep and run the rest of the way to her building on foot when he got a break. He jammed the accelerator and sped east through a yellow light.

Approaching Lynn's high-rise calmed him down. That is, until he saw her leave the building with a strange man whose arm was wrapped around her waist. He was tall and built like an athlete. Blond hair and sunglasses framed a deeply tanned face.

Throwing on the brakes, Blade stared. Was this some boyfriend she hadn't told him about?

Then he saw she didn't look at all relaxed and her body language was all wrong. Her hip was sticking out at a weird angle, as if her companion was pressing something into the small of her back.

A gun...

The bastard had a gun on her, and they were heading straight for him!

As he pulled the Jeep to the curb, Blade realized this wasn't Timothy Cooper. Nor any of the suspects on her list. Blade left the vehicle and prayed Lynn wouldn't react to seeing him. As they passed him, he meant to get the bastard without getting her hurt.

Sweat broke out over his body in anticipation. He hadn't used his finely honed skills since leaving the military. He couldn't afford to make even one mistake.

Then Lynn saw him. Her eyes went wide, but she didn't react otherwise, and he didn't think her abductor caught on. Noting the bastard's sunglasses were taped—he must have fixed them after she broke them during the original attack—Blade prepared himself mentally.

And then something shifted in the man's stance and the sunglasses turned toward him. The next thing Blade knew, the pair veered off toward the river.

Blade hurried to follow, but a group of teenagers came pouring out of a van, bouncing a basketball and blocking him.

"Out of my way!" Blade ordered.

"Hey, chill, man!" one of them said.

Another one purposely stepped in front of him and got in his face.

He shoved the kid out of his way in time to see Lynn being pushed down a set of stairs by her abductor.

LYNN NEARLY FELL ONCE, but Nathan pressed her forward, warning her that if she fell, he would shoot her right there. She believed him and cursed the fact that she had on a pair of spindly heeled sandals. The stairs went down three levels along with a network of streets, providing access to the downtown area and bridges across the Chicago River. They'd made it down two before she heard Blade's footsteps ringing above them.

"He'll catch up to us," she warned Nathan.

"Then he's dead."

"No! You can't kill him!" Abruptly, she changed her tune. "You're not a killer, Nathan," she wheedled. "You simply need professional help."

"I need Danielle, but you made sure I couldn't have her. If it wasn't for you, she would want to see me."

He was delusional, Lynn thought, but she had to play into that. "You really do need help, Nathan. Counseling. Then Dani will agree to see you," she lied.

"*You're* the problem. You just wouldn't stay put, but I found you anyway."

"How?"

"I tried to get the Jacobek woman to talk, but she wasn't any more cooperative than you. What kind of woman holds back on her new boyfriend? I got my break the night you called your parents. Star sixtynine is a very handy tool."

Lynn remembered the club phone ringing right after she'd hung up. Blade had given directions to Nathan!

"I figured out how to get Danielle back," he continued. "All I have to do is kill *you*. Once you're dead, Dani will have to come home for the funeral. And I'll be there for her, all supportive and understanding. She'll be mine again, in no time."

"Unless you get help, she won't be," Lynn retorted. "She's afraid of you."

"She was afraid of *you* and your opinion of me," Nathan countered. "That's why she left me."

But this time Lynn knew the accusation was unfounded.

They hit the bottom level running, and Nathan steered her straight into the dim reaches of the underground auto pound. A couple of city workers at the gate looked at them but immediately went back to their conversation, and a tow truck flew out the gates, the worker no doubt eager to deprive yet another motorist of his vehicle.

Glancing back over her shoulder, Lynn saw Blade come off the last set of stairs. He ran straight for them. She was torn between wanting his help and fearing for his life.

She had to do *something*...but what?

Emotionally distraught over Blade, exhausted to the bone, she hadn't been able to defend herself in the apartment. She hadn't fought Nathan when he'd forced her to leave. She'd gone docilely, resigned to her fate. But now she wasn't the only consideration.

Blade would take a bullet for you, Cass had told her.

If he did, it would be her fault. She'd made the mistake of overlooking Nathan as a suspect. She'd made another mistake coming home on her own. She'd led Blade right into a deadly trap.

I'd give my life for yours....

She believed he would.

He doesn't really die, does he?

That would be up to you....

Survival instincts, for Blade as well as herself, humming, Lynn bolted and ran between two rows of cars, figuring Nathan would lunge for her and grab her as he had before. True to form, he quickly caught up to her and clutched an arm around her middle, then whipped her in a semicircle so that she was facing Blade, who was now on the other side of the cars.

He came to a sudden halt, his wary gaze shifting to her head.

That's when Lynn felt the gun pressed to her temple, and the roar of her pulse beating through her head.

With nothing to lose, she yelled a war cry and mule-kicked and elbow-punched Nathan, and when he grunted with pain and loosened his hold, she jammed her high spiked heel down on the small bones of his foot.

He screamed in pain and let her go.

She ran straight for Blade and watched his expression change to one of horror. "Get out of the way!" she yelled. "Duck!"

"Get down!" he yelled in return, and she knew Nathan must be aiming the gun at her, but she kept running and so did Blade.

When she got close enough, Blade reached out a hand and grabbed her arm and spun her around so that he was between her and the villain, just as she knew he would. But she was ready for it. Lynn shoved Blade to the side even as Nathan fired. Blade lurched forward and blood exploded from him and splattered her.

"Oh, my God! No!" she screamed as he fell against her and slid downward, his dark eyes wide and staring. "No! Oh, God, no! Blade!"

She tried grabbing him, but the blood was slippery and coated her hands, and he fell against one of the cars and then down to the pavement.

He doesn't really die, does he?

She'd tried to save him, but she'd failed.

"Hey, what's going on?" called one of the workers.

"Murder!" she screamed, knowing Nathan wasn't the only guilty one. "Someone call the cops!"

I would give my life for yours.

Lynn sobbed. Now he had.

Glaring at Nathan, she saw red, and it was more than Blade's blood, which seemed to be everywhere.

"You won't get away with this!" she shouted.

"You won't stop me, bitch!" Nathan shrieked back.

Fury drove her forward to fight him and probably die. But he would have to kill her before she let him get away with this.

His features set in a sick smile below the taped sunglasses, he raised the gun.

But before Nathan could pull the trigger, something whooshed by her. His body arched backward and a strangled sound escaped him as blood spurted toward her once more. His hands went up to his throat and he stepped straight back into the aisle, where a city truck towing a car came roaring straight at him. Slammed hard at contact, Nathan's body went flying, limbs dancing like a puppet on strings.

When he fell back to the ground, she saw it—the knife sticking out of his throat.

Blade's knife.

With a cry of joy, Lynn turned to find the man she loved wasn't dead, after all. Then he passed out cold.

"I'VE BEEN DOING SOME thinking and have decided we're even," Lynn told Blade that night, after bringing him up to date on their attacker's true identity.

"Because I took a bullet for you?"

Shuddering at how prophetic both he and Cass had been, Lynn said, "Not exactly." Though it told her what an honorable man he was, and said a whole lot about his feelings for her, as well. "I didn't mean for you to take that bullet any more than you meant to shoot an innocent woman." She hated the fact that he was in a hospital bed because of her.

"My getting shot wasn't your fault."

"The hell it wasn't. You said you would die for me and I didn't believe you." And for an agonizing moment, she had thought he *was* dead. "My going off half-cocked set things in motion."

"I think maybe fate had a hand in those things."

"That doesn't change the fact that you got shot and could have died trying to protect me."

"But you saved me," he said. "I owe my life to you."

Thankfully, her shoving Blade at the last second probably *had* saved his life, as she'd hoped it would. The bullet had gone through his side, missing vital organs. And after Nathan had been hit by the truck, she'd returned to an unconscious Blade and had put pressure on his wound to make certain he didn't bleed to death before the paramedics arrived.

A couple of days in the hospital and Blade would be free to go home. A couple of weeks of healing time and he would be as good as new.

If only fixing their relationship could be so simple.

"It's over," he said, confirming it in her mind. "You don't have to worry about Nathan coming after you ever again."

"And Dani can come home."

While the medical examiner couldn't be sure whether the knife or being hit by the truck had killed Nathan, he was dead. Stella assured her that no charges would be brought against Blade. Still, Lynn was inexplicably saddened for Nathan, because she knew that he hadn't been purely evil. But his love had been warped. Something in his past had twisted him. If he'd gotten the help he'd needed...

But it was too late for that now.

It was too late for a lot of things.

Lynn rose from her chair. "I should go now and let you get some rest."

A hand flashed out from the bed and fastened around her wrist. "I would rest better if I knew where you were."

Her pulse fluttered under the long, warm fingers that held her fast. "I'll be at home."

"I mean personally. As in being *with* you."

He wanted to be with her? The thought made her chest hurt and her throat tighten with a lump of emotion.

"You can't leave that bed yet," she softly protested.

"Maybe not, but I could make room for you." Without letting go of her, he did just that. "The question is...do you have room for me...in your life?"

What was he asking her? Lynn's heartbeat quickened.

"You really want me to be in your life after I was so awful to you?"

"You were in shock," he said, "and you had a right to be furious with me for not telling you the truth sooner. But I love you, Lynn, and whether or not we're from two different worlds, I think we have a shot at being happy together. Now come over here."

She arched her eyebrows at him. "Is that an order?"

"Consider it an urgent request. I'm feeling faint and may need to be resuscitated at any moment."

Slipping into bed alongside the man she loved and pulling his head toward hers, she softly said, "Then it's an order I can't ignore."

Epilogue

Sitting at the bar after-hours on Blade's first night back to work, Gideon watched the man who was so much more than a bartender finesse the cork until it popped and a trail of fizz rolled down the neck of the champagne bottle.

"Don't waste it!" Cass said, laughing as she held out a flute-shaped glass.

Blade filled her glass, then four others. Each of the men took one.

"To Team Undercover," Blade said, his appreciative gaze touching Logan, Gabe, then Cass and finally Gideon. "I thank you and my lovely fiancée thanks you for helping to save her life."

"To do-overs!" Gideon added.

They all clinked glasses and sipped at the champagne, and Gideon thought this was a very good year indeed.

Not the champagne, but the actual time in his life.

Just when he'd gotten restless and had been thinking of moving on and changing identities yet again, he'd found a better use for his club, a more selfless purpose to his life. And against all odds, his old friend

Gabe Conner had found him. Gideon couldn't be more content.

"How are you and Elise doing?" he asked Logan, Elise Mitchell having been their first "case."

"We're taking it slow for the kid's sake," Logan said, referring to Elise's young son, Eric. "But we're committed, and we'll know when the time is right to let the world in on it."

Gideon joked, "Two satisfied clients, two really satisfied men." He lifted his glass to the others. "We ought to have business cards made up. 'Club Undercover. No cover charge, no identification required, secrecy guaranteed.'"

"To our next case," Cass toasted.

But then her smile dimmed and she got that look in her eyes that Gideon was starting to know all too well, making him wonder exactly what she saw in their future....

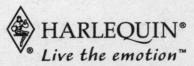

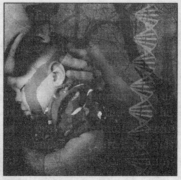
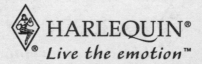

Bestselling Author

TAYLOR SMITH

On a cold winter night, someone comes looking for Grace Meade
and the key she holds to a thirty-five-year-old mystery. She is
tortured and killed, and her house is set ablaze. Incredibly,
the prime suspect is her own daughter, Jillian Meade, a woman
wanted in connection with two other murders of women Grace
knew during the war. And FBI Special Agent Alex Cruz has to find
Jillian before her past destroys her for good.

DEADLY GRACE

A "first-rate political thriller."
—*Booklist*

On sale April 2003
wherever paperbacks are sold!

Introducing an incredible new voice in romantic suspense

LAURIE BRETON

FINAL EXIT

Ten years ago tragedy tore them apart....

But when FBI Special Agent Carolyn Monahan walks back into
the life of Homicide Lieutenant Conor Rafferty, the sizzle
is undeniable. They are back together, albeit reluctantly,
to find the serial killer who is terrorizing Boston.

As the pressure builds to solve the murders, so does the attraction
between Caro and Rafferty. But the question remains:
Who will get to Caro first—the killer or the cop?

Available the first week of April 2003 wherever paperbacks are sold!

MIRA®